PRAISE FOR
THE *LIBRARY* OF *EVER*

One of *Kirkus Reviews'* Best Books of the Year

"A fast-paced adventure set in a magical library that had me smiling all the way. The main character, eleven-year-old Lenora, is the definition of 'plucky,' with her endless curiosity, strong sense of right and wrong, and take-charge attitude."

—GEEKMOM

"Reading *The Library of Ever* is like getting lost in an entire library full of books, and never wanting to leave!"

—JAMES RILEY,
New York Times–bestselling author of the Story Thieves series

"Best & Brightest Chapter Books of 2019"

—DENVER PUBLIC LIBRARY

"Best of 2019: Children's Books"

—LOS ANGELES PUBLIC LIBRARY

"The Best Books for Young Readers of 2019"

—UPENN GRADUATE SCHOOL OF EDUCATION

REBEL
❧ IN THE ❧
LIBRARY
OF EVER

ZENO ALEXANDER

{Imprint}
MAKE YOUR MARK
NEW YORK

[Imprint]
MAKE YOUR MARK

A part of Macmillan Publishing Group, LLC
120 Broadway, New York, NY 10271

REBEL IN THE LIBRARY OF EVER. Copyright © 2020 by Zeno Alexander.
All rights reserved. Printed in the United States of America by LSC
Communications, Harrisonburg, Virginia.

Library of Congress Control Number: 2019941110

ISBN 978-1-250-16919-8 (hardcover) / ISBN 978-1-250-16918-1 (ebook)

Our books may be purchased in bulk for promotional, educational, or
business use. Please contact your local bookseller or the Macmillan
Corporate and Premium Sales Department at (800) 221-7945 ext. 5442 or
by email at MacmillanSpecialMarkets@macmillan.com.

Book design by Ellen Duda

Imprint logo designed by Amanda Spielman

First edition, 2020

1   3   5   7   9   10   8   6   4   2

mackids.com

To steal this book, if you should try,
It's by your toes you will hang high.
And ravens then will gather 'bout
To find your eyes and pluck them out.
And when you're screaming, "No, no, no!"
Remember, you deserved this woe.

To those who shine a light

CONTENTS

CONTENTS

CHAPTER ONE
Lenora Returns

Lenora was bruised and battered.

She slumped against the wall of the dojo in her uniform and mask, feeling utterly beaten. Everything ached. Everyone else at the kendo dojo was much older, taller, and stronger than Lenora, not to mention much more experienced in the Japanese martial art of sword-fighting. Battling them was hopeless. And she could tell they were taking it easy on her, too, which only made her get angrier and fight harder.

Even getting into the class had been a struggle.

"I'm sorry," the sensei, a very nice old man, had said when she'd first showed up. "But we don't have enough interested children to start a children's class."

I don't want *a children's class,* Lenora almost snarled, then stopped herself. The teacher meant well, after all. "I need to study kendo, sensei," she told him, bowing. "I need to become a master, because—" She hesitated. She couldn't tell him the true reason. He would never believe her, any more than her parents had.

"I got a job at the library!" she'd announced to her parents with excitement after her return from her first adventures at the otherworldly library that spanned all of space and time.

"I told you, Lenora," her father had said. "Libraries don't hire eleven-year-olds."

"But it's true," she said. "And there were spaceships, and I shrank to the size of an ant, and . . ." She stopped. Her parents were staring at her with alarm.

"That's . . . fascinating, dear," her mother said with concern. "You've always had such a vivid imagination. Maybe you should write this all down. We could show it to a nice doctor."

After that, Lenora had learned to keep silent about the Library—for that was how she thought of it now, with a capital L, and its name "not written in ink but in a golden splash," to quote one of Lenora's favorite books.

"Because," she had said to the sensei, "I—I— really like kendo. Please let me try." Lenora winced at her weak response. But she could not tell the truth.

The sensei had pondered this, chin in hand, looking Lenora up and down. "I would not normally do this," he said. "But there is something about you . . . I will allow you to try. It will be very difficult, you know."

Lenora was not worried about that. If only the teacher knew how very many difficult things she had already overcome.

Now, a year later, as she leaned against the wall, her entire body begging for mercy, the sensei approached and removed his mask. He smiled at her kindly, and, she could tell with irritation, a bit of pity. "I admire your fighting spirit, Lenora," he said. "But this really isn't the place for a twelve-year-old."

"I must study kendo, sensei," she told him, bowing despite her aches and pains. "I need to become a master, because years in the future, I'm going to have to fight off three robots wielding two swords each in pitch darkness, and I need to be ready."

"I see," said the sensei, putting his mask back on. "Well, back at it, then." He returned to the group of fighters whirling about, shouting and hitting one another with their bamboo swords. Over the past year, the sensei had gotten quite used to the occasional odd phrase slipping through Lenora's lips, and they had developed a silent agreement that he would not ask any further questions.

Lenora thought about returning to the fray. But she had to admit to herself that she had had enough for one night. Her parents had been completely mystified as to why Lenora had demanded to take kendo classes six nights a week, but they had finally agreed. They were also confused as to why she wanted to spend her remaining free hours after

school at the library, reading, but after much argu-
ing and pleading from Lenora they had allowed her
to take the bus by herself so that she could go any-
time she wanted.

Lenora had tried to get back to the Library. She
had searched every inch of the regular library with
its lovely, large windows through which sunlight
poured eagerly in, and beautiful cedar beams that
stretched up to the high ceiling. But she hadn't
found a way in. She'd asked the librarians, but
they would only smile mysteriously and change the
subject. So Lenora knew she'd have to be patient,
however much she hated that.

She knew that when she *did* get back, she had
to be ready. Ready not only to help her patrons,
but to fight the Forces of Darkness, who were the
enemies of knowledge and wore black bowler hats
and would try to devour her the first chance they
got. She'd faced them several times before, and the
experiences had been so harrowing that she still
jumped every time a person in a black hat passed
her on the street.

And so Lenora could only read book after book

after book, and get herself whacked around by kendo swords, and wait as a year passed.

One Saturday morning she was lying in her favorite spot at the library, a window seat that was sunny all day long, reading about the Battle of Pelusium and wondering if it really *had* been fought with cats. She'd met a time traveler in the Library who might be able to tell her, and resolved to ask him the next time she saw him.

The library had been oddly quiet all morning. Lenora realized it had been a long time since she'd seen any patrons, or any librarians. Closing her book, she got up to investigate. She went out into the wide-open atrium at the center of the library and looked in all directions. She didn't see anyone, not even any librarians behind the reference desk.

Then a librarian swerved into view, walking swiftly from the back of the building. As the woman got closer, Lenora saw she was crying and carrying a cardboard box. Lenora ran to her. Her name was Aaliyah, and she was one of Lenora's favorites. "What's wrong?" Lenora asked, alarmed.

Aaliyah stopped, sniffling. "I've been fired," she said through her tears.

"What?" said Lenora, outraged. "Whyever would they fire you?" For Aaliyah, in Lenora's expert opinion, was one of the best.

Aaliyah looked in all directions. It was as though she suspected someone was watching or listening to them. Then she beckoned Lenora off to the side, into a narrow space between two stacks. She looked around again, then knelt and whispered into Lenora's ear: "The Library needs you. You have to hurry!" And from the way she said it, Lenora knew exactly which Library she meant.

Then Aaliyah stood, took one more fearful look around, and moved to leave.

"Wait!" said Lenora in a loud whisper. "Don't leave. Stay and fight! I'll find a way to save your job, I promise."

Lenora knew that if she had said such a thing to any other adult, they would have simply patted her on her head and called her adorable.

But not Aaliyah. Aaliyah was a librarian. And she knew.

The woman put her box on the floor. "Very well," she said in a whisper. "I will try. But I don't know how long I can manage. Please hurry, Lenora!"

And then she strode quickly away, toward one of the deepest corners of this library.

Lenora stood there, stunned. *The Library needs you.* But why? And what could she do to help? She had no idea even how to get back to it.

While she stood there, she noticed a woman and a boy approach the reference desk and look around curiously, doubtless wondering why there wasn't a librarian in sight.

There was nothing else for Lenora to do. She strode over to the desk and went behind it, her heart pounding with excitement at being back behind a reference desk.

"Hello," said Lenora. "How may I help you?"

The lady peered down her nose at Lenora. "Aren't you a little young to work here?"

"Try me," replied Lenora.

"Well," said the woman, hesitating.

The boy spoke up. "I need to know what the world's largest number is."

"I already told him the largest number is infinity," said the woman. "But he won't listen."

"Infinity isn't really a number," said Lenora. She'd gotten deeply into the math section that fall.

"Of course it is," said the woman. "Everyone knows that. I want to speak to a real librarian."

Lenora drew herself up to her full height, which admittedly wasn't much. She wished she were ten feet tall like Chief Answerer Malachi, the imposing woman who had given Lenora her job at the Library along with several most interesting assignments. Malachi could have looked down her nose at this woman instead of peering up at her from below, as Lenora was forced to do. "I *am* a real librarian, and infinity is *not* the world's largest number."

"If you're a real librarian," challenged the woman, "then where is your badge?"

Lenora was crushed. Her badge, which listed many of her greatest accomplishments at the Library, had vanished upon her departure a year ago. She still had her library card, which she wore on a string around her neck next to her heart, where it glowed faintly and even hummed from time to time (she had no idea why), but the badge was gone.

"I left it in the staff room," lied Lenora. "I'll get it and I'll get the answer to your question." Maybe another librarian had left a badge lying around and Lenora could use that. She didn't feel this was a deception. She really *was* a librarian, and an excellent one at that. Also, she didn't like the woman and wanted to help the boy get the right answer.

The staff room was right behind the reference desk. She marched in. The room had comfortable-looking tables and chairs and a counter with a sink and small microwave oven. There were some desks, too, but no badges to be seen. She went farther in. In the back there were some shelves, rather messily organized, with stacks of papers and journals and books and supplies. She dashed through the shelves, looking everywhere for a badge. But there was none to be found. The woman would never believe her, and the boy would not get the right answer. There was no worse feeling for Lenora.

Somehow she seemed to have gotten turned

around. There had only been a few shelves, but no matter which way she turned, she kept coming back to them. She couldn't find the area with the tables and sink and microwave.

She was lost. A thrill ran through her. This had happened before, and . . . was it possible?

Lenora realized her library card was humming. She pulled it out from beneath her shirt. It was blazing with glorious light, the words LIBRARY CARD glittering with all the colors of the rainbow, and it was fluttering about like a butterfly. Lenora grasped hold of it tightly.

She remembered the words of her much older, future self, Lenora the kendo master, who had given Lenora the library card and said: *When the time comes, you will need this. Don't worry, you'll know.*

Lenora needed this. Hoping against hope, she did the only thing she could think of. She gripped the card, closed her eyes, and whispered the phrase whose meaning she had learned when clutched in the very grip of the Forces, within their cold, impenetrable dark:

"Knowledge Is a Light."

There was a tremendous crack, like a granite boulder splitting open. Lenora opened her eyes, and there, to her great delight, was a massive stone archway in the wall where none had been before, above which a phrase had been deeply chiseled:

KNOWLEDGE IS A LIGHT

Shrieking with joy, Lenora raced through the archway and into the tunnel beyond. Though as she did, she noticed something was different. She had seen these words before, so sharply chiseled, but now they looked weathered and worn, as though no one had been maintaining them for ages. But it didn't matter, she was back in the Library, and she couldn't be more excited.

Her excitement ended when she reached the end of the tunnel.

CHAPTER TWO
Lenora Learns

Lenora looked forward to seeing the Library again, with its vast and dazzling towers, endless stacks of books, giant windows with infinite vistas beyond, and blimps and tubes and talking whales and whatever other marvels the Library might toss her way.

But this did not happen.

The tunnel ended in the most depressing, low-ceilinged room, cramped with completely empty bookshelves shoved together haphazardly, with horrid neon bulbs flickering dismally above. The floor was dirty tile and all the whitish walls were bare.

Lenora took a deep breath, steadying herself. This was nothing like the dreams she'd been having of her magnificent return to the Library. She had all the information she needed to know that something was Terribly Wrong.

Then she felt a fluttering on her chest, right in front of her heart. She looked down to see that a badge had appeared there, and the badge said

LENORA

◆——◦⦂◦——◆

SECOND APPRENTICE LIBRARIAN

This was unimaginably reassuring. Despite things being Terribly Wrong, she had her badge back, she was still a librarian, and she had a job to do. And judging from her new title, she'd even gotten a promotion from Third Apprentice, her final title when she had last been in the Library. She hoped that meant she wouldn't be fired somehow, like Aaliyah had been. Steeling herself for whatever was to come, she looked around for an exit—for she knew the first thing she had to do was locate Chief Answerer Malachi and find out what was going on.

She wandered through the shelves, noting that none of them were the least bit dusty, and so must have been emptied recently. At last she came to a door, which she pushed open to find a long hallway lined with more doors, and more dirty tile and flickering lights. It all looked like a scene from those television shows about adults who hate their jobs, and Lenora was beginning to wonder if she was actually in the Library at all.

She was disappointed to see no sign of a Tube station, the tubes being the main means of travel through the vast Library, whooshing librarians along in glass tubes that could take them almost anywhere. But then she remembered she no longer had a Tube key, and so she could not use the system even if she wanted to.

There was nowhere to go but forward, so forward she went.

As she passed, she could see all the doors were open, and beyond each was a small office with nothing in it but a beat-up desk and chair. After about ten or twelve of these, Lenora jumped a little when she passed one with a woman sitting in it. The woman was sitting at the desk with hands folded, staring at the wall. She was wearing a red raincoat on which was a badge that said LIBRARIAN with no name. She turned her head slowly to look at Lenora. Something behind her eyes flickered. And beneath that raincoat, a snake-like something slithered over her shoulder.

Goose bumps rose on Lenora's arms, and she knew. The Forces of Darkness. The flickering and slithering told her, but somehow, she knew that she would have recognized this creature for what it was even without those things. Perhaps she would think about that later, because the woman had already stood and was stalking toward her.

Lenora was a girl of action. She had learned to venture forth boldly and rely on her wits and valor. But somehow, she could not move. Her feet felt bolted to the floor. Sweat broke out all over her and she began to shake. In the most dangerous moments, Lenora had always kept her head. But now she was simply terrified. She felt, rising within her, a scream.

The woman came close and leaned over, studying Lenora's eyes. "Who are you?" she asked in a voice that sent more waves of terror through Lenora. *Run!* her mind begged. But she could not.

"I—I'm a librarian," Lenora squeaked, humiliated at the sound of her own voice.

"How nice," the woman said. Something wriggled beneath her coat. "But I have not seen you before. Perhaps you do not know that librarians are not so welcome here these days. You may choose to quit, be fired, or cooperate. If you do none of those things, we will, of course, eat you. Choose. Now."

Lenora had heard such a threat before. *I say we eat her now and get it over with,* a monster like this woman had once said about Lenora. She closed her eyes, remembering that moment, and what Malachi had told her afterward: *Knowledge Is a Light, Lenora.* Everything Malachi had said at the time was forever etched in Lenora's mind, as though chiseled in stone: *Throughout history, that light has at times burned very dimly, and nearly even gone out, while in other times it has blazed up gloriously.*

As she remembered those words, she was surprised to hear a sudden hiss. She opened her eyes, and was shocked to see the woman flinching back, away from Lenora. For the briefest moment, she looked down at her hands. Was she glowing, as she had glowed once before? There seemed to be something, barely visible under the harsh light . . . but there was no time to think about it. All her fear had vanished, and she could move again. But already the woman in the raincoat was recovering.

Lenora wasted no time in breaking into a full run. In her career the Forces had made any number of attempts to squish or eat or attack her with swords, and she wasn't about to wait around to find out what this one, who was more terrifying than all the rest put together, would do.

Suddenly, she found herself at an intersection of eight hallways going in all directions, all of them seemingly endless and identical to the one Lenora had come down. She whirled to see if the woman in the red raincoat was chasing her, but no one was there.

Then a door burst open a few yards down another corridor, and a man rushed out, his arms full of books. He looked in both directions, then ran toward the intersection. He seemed quite out of breath, with a flushed face and drips of sweat running down his temples. And he had a badge that Lenora could make out as he came closer:

PAOLO

———— ⁘ ————

ASSISTANT TO THE ASSISTANT ANSWERER

Lenora knew that this was a real librarian. She could tell with a glance, though she still didn't know how. Perhaps it came with her promotion. At any rate, she quickly surmised that if Paolo was the Assistant to the Assistant Answerer, then he could tell her where the Assistant Answerer was, and that person could tell her where the Chief Answerer, Malachi, was. And so even though Paolo was about to run right past her, she put out a hand and cried "Wait!"

Paolo stopped instantly, nearly dropping all his books, which were really too many for one person to try to carry at a run.

Lenora could tell he was in a hurry (who couldn't?), so she spoke quickly. "Where is the Assistant Answerer?"

The man's eyes widened in alarm. He looked up at the ceiling, then in all eight directions, before looking back at Lenora and, awkwardly, putting one finger to his lips. Lenora caught two of his books as they fell.

Paolo pointed down one of the hallways, then reached for the books. Lenora handed them back silently. She wanted to offer to help him with whatever was wrong, but he had indicated silence, and so she said nothing. Once he had the books, he took off running in another direction.

Lenora went down the hallway she'd been pointed toward. She walked past one door after another, until she reached one with a placard that read ASSISTANT ANSWERER. The door was closed. She raised one hand to knock, but before she could, a voice spoke from behind the door.

"Come in, Lenora."

The voice was Malachi's.

CHAPTER THREE
Lenora Listens

Lenora threw open the door. "Malachi!" she
cried to the dark-skinned woman, before paus-
ing to take in the scene.

She had never seen the Chief Answerer's office
before (and wasn't sure that Malachi had ever had
or needed one in the past), but this did not seem
at all like a place Malachi would choose to work.
It was little different from the other small offices
she'd seen, except that there were floor-to-ceiling
bookshelves covering the walls, all groaning under

the weight of hundreds of books. Lenora sighed with relief at the sight of the first proper bookshelves she'd seen since entering the Library.

The desk was just the same as the desks she'd seen elsewhere, and so naturally it was far too small for the ten-foot-tall Chief Answerer. Her head, with its perfect bun held in place with two ever-so-sharp pencils, almost brushed the ceiling even though she was sitting in her little chair, her knees poking up higher than Lenora's head. Down the length of her sharp nose she peered at Lenora, and if Lenora didn't know better she'd think there might be a twitch of a smile at one end of her lips.

"It is good to see you, Lenora," she said primly. "And I see you've grown."

That was true. Lenora, always the shortest in her class, had undergone something of a growth spurt lately, and was now perhaps only the fifth- or sixth-shortest. But Malachi often said things that had more than one meaning, and Lenora suspected this was one of them.

Then she saw it, and gasped. Malachi's badge. It read, against all sense:

MALACHI

————— ·:· —————

ASSISTANT ANSWERER

"*Assistant* Answerer!" cried Lenora. "But—" And then she was instantly silenced by Malachi's long finger going to her lips.

The Chief—Assistant?—Answerer pointed slowly to all four corners of the ceiling, then pointed to her ears, then back. Lenora understood immediately what she'd begun to guess from Paolo.

Someone was listening. And so Lenora must be very careful what she said.

Malachi spoke in a rather flat tone unlike her usual speech. "It's quite simple, Lenora. There is new leadership on the Board."

The Board! Lenora had heard that term right before she left the Library the first time. But she still had no idea what it was.

"The Board determined that the Library needed to

modernize," Malachi continued. "Needed outside-the-box thinking and innovation. Synergy. Paradigms."

Again, Lenora had no idea what Malachi was talking about. But she suspected, strongly, that Malachi was simply speaking for whoever was listening and didn't believe a word of it herself.

"And they brought in a new Director to run the Library. He had, as we were told, a vision. A very *great* vision."

Malachi leaned into the word *great* with such force that Lenora almost took a step back.

"And so there has been a reorganization. My duties have been . . . changed . . . in keeping with the vision. Many librarians, who were no longer a good"—and here Malachi paused, closed her eyes, and took a deep breath—"*fit*, were offered the opportunity to seek new jobs elsewhere. Away from the Library."

(*I've been fired,* Lenora remembered the weeping Aaliyah telling her earlier.)

"New librarians have been hired as well." Malachi looked at her intently. "Some of them you have met before."

Lenora understood, though she almost collapsed at the thought that the Forces of Darkness were working as "librarians" now.

"But one must adapt, Lenora. There is still much work to be done. In fact, there is more to be done than ever before."

Lenora was not sure what she could say and what she couldn't, so she asked tentatively, "What should I do, then?"

"As it happens, you've shown up at exactly the right time. I have an extremely important task, and therefore you are precisely the right librarian to handle it."

Lenora's heart swelled at the words, but she was worried she might let Malachi down. After all, she still did not fully understand what was going on.

"I would like you to go to the Philosophy section as quickly as possible. There, you will find a girl, ten years of age. It is vital that you help her."

Then Malachi reached out her palm, revealing a familiar object—a metal fob the size of a domino, dangling from a necklace. A Tube key. Lenora took the necklace and with great solemnity put it over her head, leaving the key to dangle just next to her badge. Then Malachi opened a drawer and removed an object that Lenora knew quite well— her old notebook! She grasped it eagerly and flipped through, seeing that all her notes were still there. She dropped the notebook into one of the large pockets that she had begun insisting be included on all her dresses, along with a couple of sharp pencils from a box on the desk.

While Lenora did this, Malachi wrote something on a piece of paper. (Her desk was neatly arranged with several stacks.)

She held up the paper to Lenora. On it Lenora read:

YOU MUST REMEMBER THREE THINGS. THE FIRST IS YOUR OATH.

Lenora remembered. *Do you swear to follow the librarian's oath? Do you swear to work hard? Do you swear to venture forth bravely and find the answer to any question, no matter the challenge? Do you swear to find a path for those who are lost, and to improvise and think on your feet and rely on your wits and valor? And, do you swear to oppose the enemies of knowledge with all your courage and strength, wherever they might be found?*

She had given a solemn "I do" to every question, then done her very best to stay true to her promise.

Next was this:

THE SECOND THING—NEVER LIE TO HER, LENORA. NO MATTER

HOW MUCH EASIER IT MIGHT MAKE THINGS IN THE TIMES

AHEAD, ALWAYS TELL HER THE TRUTH.

Lenora said nothing, but gave a firm nod, which Malachi returned just as firmly. Though Lenora did not know exactly who "her" was, it seemed very likely it was this mysterious girl in the Philosophy section.

And finally:

THIRD: HELP ZENODOTUS!

Lenora had no idea who that was either, and though she wanted desperately to ask, she knew she could not.

"Now go," said Malachi. "Make a left and head all the way to the end of this hallway. You'll find a door that says DO NOT ENTER. Go through that and you'll find a Tube station nearby."

Lenora nodded, and knowing there was, as usual, no time to waste, dashed out of the office and down the hallway at a dead run.

CHAPTER FOUR
Lenora Leans In

Lenora was nearly out of breath, wondering if this hallway would go on forever, when she finally saw the door marked DO NOT ENTER at the end. And when she pushed through she knew she was back in the real Library at last.

She was on a high balcony overlooking a long room that went farther into the distance than she could see. Its floor was divided into lanes of water, sort of like a swimming pool for racing, but the lanes were divided by solid floors in which massive metal gears were set. The gears churned slowly, for what purpose Lenora could not say. The lanes of water had gondolas moving along them. Most were empty, but a few were steered by librarians holding long paddles, and had books piled in them.

To her left, she heard the familiar whooshing sounds coming from what could only be a Tube station. She turned and noticed something even stranger than this room. Where before there had been bookshelves, now all along the walls were computer monitors, dozens upon dozens of them. And all of them were showing the same thing—a pasty-faced yet handsome man in an expensive-looking suit and tie, a man with perfect salt-and-pepper hair who looked as though he might have stepped off a movie screen. He seemed to be giving a speech. Lenora listened.

". . . as you can see from the changes around you, I've been keeping my promises as Director. The Library is making money for the first time . . ."

Making money? thought Lenora. Libraries didn't exist to make money. And then a tremor went through her. The man's voice . . .

". . . and patron fees for Library use have been lowered under my leadership . . ."

Lenora recoiled. *Patron fees?* Patrons had never paid fees. Libraries were free! And she was beginning to remember where she had heard this voice before, talking about the Library making money . . .

". . . as we continue to trim down our excessive and expensive book collection . . ."

And Lenora remembered.

His voice.

She'd heard him through a listening tube before, talking over Malachi and interrupting the Chief Answerer whenever she tried to speak:

. . . *The Library simply isn't making money* . . . (Lenora remembered well Malachi's reply, that the value of libraries could not be counted in money) . . . *run it like a business . . . get rid of the unprofitable books* . . .

Now Lenora knew who Malachi must have been speaking to. The Director. The man on the monitors.

She shook herself, realizing that she had no time for this mystery quite yet. She had to get to the Philosophy section as quickly as possible. So off she flew in the direction of the whooshing Tube station.

As she ran, she heard snatches of conversation from various patrons, to her dismay:

"The Library is changing, but he says he's making it better . . ."

"Making money is good, isn't it? But I do wonder how people will pay their fees . . ."

"He seems to know what he's doing, though it is a bit harder to find books these days . . ."

But then she reached the Tube station, and her heart leapt at the sight of the old familiar tubes, wonderful as could be—giant, rugged glass cylinders, bound in rings of sturdy copper, capsules within them shooting past, whisking librarians to their destinations all through the vast Library.

The hair on the back of her neck prickled. Something was wrong. Lenora looked around. There was one other librarian waiting for a tube. A tall, tall man in a heavy black overcoat that went down over his shoes, whose head was slowing turning toward Lenora. In one hand he held a basketful of books and in the other a box of matches.

This was not a librarian. She could somehow simply sense it, the prickly feeling no accident. The man was now staring straight at her, and something slithered up the side of his leg, under his coat. Lenora headed straight for a tube on the other side of the station, head high and chin up, ignoring him completely. When a capsule arrived, she hopped up the steps and began to climb in. Just then, the man called out to her.

"We've won, you know. It's over."

A chill went through Lenora, but she neither paused nor responded. Relief washed over her as she settled into the usual single, reclining seat, with its lovely cracked leather upholstery, and the door to the capsule closed firmly. Lenora considered the capsule's interior. There were thousands of slots all around her, each labeled with the name of a destination in the Library. She scanned them for the one that said Philosophy. She was disturbed to see that a large number of the slots, which normally all had brightly lit labels, had gone dark, and she resolved to look into that mystery as well, as soon as she could. At last she located Philosophy, thankful to see it was still lit, and plunged her key in straightaway.

The capsule shooshed off, the force pushing Lenora back into her seat.

The trip seemed to take longer than normal. Lenora wondered if something was Terribly Wrong with the tubes, too. And the entire journey took place in darkness. Normally Lenora was able to see new bits of the Library as she sped along (she still meant to visit that ice cave from last time whenever she could), but this time she couldn't see anything outside the glass besides pitch darkness.

However, the tube eventually slowed, her chair swiveling around in the other direction as she was again pushed back in her seat. The capsule came into the station, and light returned. The door slid open and Lenora exited to find, with much relief, that it had delivered her to the correct place: a massive stone arch with the word PHILOSOPHY carved above. In she went.

As soon as she entered, an elderly woman hobbled rapidly over, moving with surprising speed for someone who used a cane. "Oh my, at last!" she said. "A librarian! I've been searching and searching for one. Can you help me, please?"

Lenora was torn. On the one hand, she had to find that girl. On the other, she had vowed to help all those with questions. Hoping this was an easy one, she replied, "Yes, of course. How may I help you?"

"Oh, thank you," the woman said with a tremendous sigh of relief. "You see, several of my friends and I have pooled our money and bought an island. We plan to set up our own society there, but we don't quite know how to go about it. I'm looking for a copy of Plato's *Republic*."

"For ideas on how to set up a just, happy society," said Lenora. "Of course." With confidence (for this was an easy one), she led the woman down the correct row (she'd spent enough time in one library or another at this point that she could find most books with ease). But there was something strange about the shelves. Instead of books by and about people like Socrates, Rousseau, Al-Farabi, Confucius, Arendt, Leibniz, and Hildegard of Bingen, there were books by only one person.

The Director.

His face glowed out from every cover, with a smile that seemed just a bit too huge. There were dozens of different titles, so many that Lenora had serious doubts he had really written all of them. They had titles that had nothing to do with philosophy, like *How to Get Incredibly Rich* and *How to Make Unbelievable Amounts of Money* (Lenora wondered what was missing from the first book if he still had to write the second). She and the elderly lady walked past *How to Be the Best at Everything* and *How to Be Smarter than Everyone Except Me* and *Why I Am the Greatest*.

Plato's *Republic* was nowhere to be found.

Crestfallen, Lenora turned to the woman. "I'm sorry," she said, her heart breaking. "We don't seem to have a copy." She could not describe how very awful she felt at that moment.

The woman's face fell. "Oh," she said. "Well, thank you for trying, dear. I suppose we'll just have to make do." And with that, she hobbled off.

Lenora nearly burst into tears. But she managed to hold them in, because she had to find that girl. And, turning around, she did.

A pasty-faced girl who appeared to be ten years of age was walking along the stacks farther down. She was dressed in the oddest way, with a multi-colored scarf around her neck, a pink shirt covered in sparkles, and green pants that had been stitched with flowers. On her feet she wore enormous velvet platform shoes that made her, annoyingly, almost as tall as Lenora. Lenora hurried toward her. As she did, she could see the girl had a smile on her face as she looked at one book after the next.

Catching up at last, Lenora said, rather breathlessly, "Hello. How may I help you?"

The girl turned to her, beaming. "Oh, I don't need any help."

"You don't?" said Lenora in surprise. Did she have the wrong girl?

"No," said the girl. "I'm just admiring the books."

"Admiring them? Why?"

"Because," said the girl brightly, "my daddy wrote them all!"

CHAPTER FIVE
Lenora Counts

"Your *father* is the Director?" Lenora gasped.

"Yep!" announced the girl with obvious pride.

"I see," said Lenora. She didn't want to say anything about her opinion of the Director to this girl, who seemed so happy and proud, so instead she said, "Are you sure you don't need any help? The Chief—I mean, the Assistant Answerer told me you did."

"Nope," said the girl. "Although . . . I suppose

I'm a little bored. There's not much to do around here."

Not much to do in the Library?!? thought Lenora. Then again, since so many books had been replaced by screens showing the Director giving speeches, the girl might be right. And Malachi had told her to help the girl, so perhaps giving her something interesting to do was exactly what the Chief . . . rather, Assistant Answerer meant.

"How about you come with me, then?" Lenora said. "I've got a patron who needs to know what the largest number is. You can help me find out."

"The largest number is infinity," said the girl.

"Infinity's not really a number," said Lenora. "It's more complicated than that."

"Really?" said the girl, putting her fist to her chin as though deep in thought. "We could just ask Daddy. He knows everything."

"Maybe," said Lenora hurriedly, "but don't you think it might be more *fun* to find out ourselves? Finding answers around this place generally is."

The girl brightened. "That's a great idea! Okay! But I—" And then she stopped.

Lenora, somehow, knew exactly why. She turned around slowly to see a young woman, dressed in a suit—but it was not a young woman at all, Lenora knew. And she was glaring at Lenora with a twisted face.

"Princess," said the "woman" in a voice dripping with bile, "you are to come with me immediately. And you are not to associate with this—girl—ever again."

Princess? thought Lenora.

Princess stomped one of her extremely large platform shoes. "I'm not going anywhere with you! I'm going with her and we're going on a mission to find out—"

"A secret mission . . ." muttered Lenora.

"To—to find out something," Princess finished weakly.

The woman fixed Lenora with a vile look that felt like it could punch a hole in the wall, but Lenora held her ground. She'd seen worse, and she responded with a firm and calm face that let the woman know exactly that.

"The Director will hear about this," snapped

the woman, and with a whoosh of air and a popping sound, she vanished.

Princess shivered. "I don't like those people."

"Neither do I," replied Lenora, which hardly covered it.

"But don't worry," Princess said. "They all work for Daddy, and Daddy gives me anything I want. They won't hurt us."

Lenora was not so sure about that, not so sure about that at all. She thought it would be a very good idea to get out of there as quickly as possible. But first—

"Princess?" Lenora said. "Princess of what?"

"Oh, I'm not a princess," said Princess. "That's just what Daddy always calls me, and so everyone else does, too."

"Well, I'm not calling you Princess," said Lenora. "What's your real name?"

"I hate my real name," said the girl.

"Then pick something else," said Lenora. "Just be quick about it. I don't think we should stick around here much longer."

"*Anything?*" said the girl, smiling wide. "Wow.

No one ever let me do that before, no matter how much I complained! How about . . . how about Lucy? She's my favorite character from the book I read."

The *book you've read?* thought Lenora. This girl had read only one book? Lenora had so many questions, but now was not the time. Taking Lucy by the hand, she headed for the Tube station, and the girl came along eagerly.

Luckily, Lucy was small enough that she could squeeze into the cracked leather seat right beside Lenora. Lenora scanned the slots, hoping that the one she wanted hadn't gone dark. But then she found it, and slid her key into place.

"Googology?" said Lucy as the tube took off with a swoosh. "What's that?"

"The study of large numbers," said Lenora. "I figure that's the place to start."

CHAPTER SIX
Lenora in the Dark

Lenora and Lucy sped through the darkness outside the tube toward Googology. Lenora did not like this darkness at all. A thought came to her: *The lamps are going out all over the Library.* This was something Lenora had read about Europe at the beginning of the First World War—a man had said, *The lamps are going out.* The second part of the quote went: *We shall not see them lit again in our lifetime.* Lenora was determined that this part would not come true. Knowledge Is a Light, she knew, and that Light would return to the Library if she had anything to say about it.

They arrived, and as both girls went under the archway into Googology, Lenora was surprised to see that there was nothing here but a large, round room with a domed ceiling, and nothing to do with large numbers anywhere in sight. In the middle of the floor, however, was a big circular hole. She walked to the edge and looked down, Lucy right beside her.

"What is *that*?" Lucy asked.

Lenora thought for a moment. Quite obviously, it was a slide, and one that spiraled down and down to a destination she could not see. But this slide was made of something very strange, and yet somehow familiar from the many math books she'd read, and after a moment she snapped her fingers. "A slide rule."

"A slide what?"

Lenora pointed. "See how the slide is all covered with numbers? And there's a bar in the middle that slides back and forth. Or at least it could, before the slide rule got turned into a slide."

"So it's a ruler," said Lucy.

"Not quite," replied Lenora. "A slide rule was a computer you could operate by hand. You could use it for division and multiplication, and also for functions such as roots, exponents, trigonometry, logarithms . . ."

"Uh, what?"

Lenora shook her head. "Don't worry about it for now. I'll lend you a copy of *Computers: The First Two Thousand Years* later. The important thing is that they were used for centuries to do a lot of work that people would use electronic computers for later. Knowing the Library, this is probably the world's longest slide rule, and once it wasn't needed anymore, some clever librarian turned the slide rule into a slide."

"So what do we do now?"

"What do you think?" said Lenora, and hopped onto the slide. She immediately found herself shooting down the dizzying spiral, all kinds of digits flashing around on all sides (she even spotted a π), as though she'd been caught up in a tornado of numbers.

She twisted around and saw that Lucy had followed her, her face covered in unbridled glee. *This is rather fun,* Lenora thought. She'd been so caught up in her serious worries about the Library that she'd forgotten about all the fun she had promised Lucy. So she lay back and whooped with delight, and so did Lucy.

Down and down they spun, shrieking and laughing, until the slide's steep slope grew more gradual, and then finally flattened out entirely and they both came to a giggling stop.

"Phew," said Lenora, sitting up. "I needed that." But then she said nothing more, for she was stunned by what she saw before her.

Stretching far out in front of them was the longest room Lenora had ever seen, and that was saying something. The room was well lit at the beginning, where the girls sat, but there were fewer and fewer lights as the very tall shelves continued down (Lenora was relieved to see actual books on them), until in the far distance all she could see was total darkness. Utter silence surrounded them and they were completely alone. This was a bit eerie, but Lenora could sense no presence of the Forces of Darkness (*How can I do that?* she wondered). The darkness far away down this long room was only ordinary darkness, nothing more.

She stood and took a few steps toward the row of shelves, marveling at the books stacked on them. They were like no books she'd seen before. They made the huge book she'd once found in History of Science look like a matchbox in comparison. Some of them seemed to be as tall as Malachi, others dozens or hundreds of feet tall. They'd be utterly impossible to read, and if one of them contained the world's largest number, there was absolutely no way she'd ever be able to lend it to that boy. She continued forward, pondering, when she suddenly heard a clomping rush of feet and then found Lucy cowering beside her, clutching Lenora's hand, her face white as could be.

"What's wrong?" asked Lenora.

"This is scary!" whispered Lucy shakily.

Lenora looked at the long, dark hall. She supposed this was rather scary, but after the things she had seen, the thought had not occurred to her.

"There, there," she said soothingly, patting Lucy's hand. "There's nothing bad here." At least, nothing as bad as the Forces. What else there might be, she couldn't say. Then she remembered Malachi's instructions never to lie to the girl. She corrected herself quickly. "There's nothing as bad as those people who work for your father, anyway."

"Daddy would never hire anyone bad," objected Lucy, bristling a little. "They're just . . . creepy."

Lenora decided to leave that alone for now. "Well, if there is any danger, don't worry. I plan to protect you." And that was very much true.

Then they both jumped a foot in the air when a voice out of nowhere said, "Hello. How may I help you?"

CHAPTER SEVEN
Lenora and O

Lenora tried to spin around and look everywhere for the source of the voice, which was somewhat difficult, as Lucy was clinging to her and shrieking her head off. For a moment she thought this might be another invisible memory, like the spectral girl she'd met in the Library of Forgotten Knowledge. But then she saw it—a slight shimmering, hardly visible, floating in the air beside them.

"Shh, shh," Lenora said to Lucy, patting her on the back. "It's just a librarian." Though she had no idea what kind of librarian this was, she simply knew it was, just like she knew a member of the Forces on the spot.

Lucy stopped shrieking and sniffed. "Where?"

Lenora pointed to the shimmering. "Right there."

Lucy looked. "I don't see anything."

"Hmm," said Lenora. "Well, you'll have to trust me." And then, to the shimmering, she said, "It's nice to meet you. May I ask your name?" For this librarian had no visible badge.

"I am ○," said the shimmering, and Lucy yelped again at what Lenora supposed must seem like a voice coming from absolutely nothing.

"Excuse me?" said Lenora, for she could not quite understand the name the shimmering had used.

"○," said the voice again. "But I suppose that might be difficult for you to say. I am one of the new Chinese characters introduced by Empress Wu Zetian, the only woman ever to reign over China, in 689. Originally, I meant 'star,' but nowadays people mostly use me to mean 'zero,' which is rather disappointing."

"Perhaps we can just call you Star, then?" inquired Lenora.

"That would be lovely," sighed Star.

Lenora could see that Lucy was still trembling. *Poor thing,* thought Lenora. Obviously this type of experience was quite new to her. "Star," she asked, "is it possible you could make yourself visible to my friend?"

"Oh, yes," replied Star, and immediately an ○ the size of a large dinner plate was floating in front of them.

"Wow!" yelped Lucy, dropping Lenora's hand immediately. "Who . . . what . . . how?!?"

"It is rather complicated," replied Star. "Perhaps if we had a few months, I could explain."

"Unfortunately, we actually have very little time at the moment," said Lenora.

"Well, maybe later," said Lucy, her voice full of longing.

Lenora wanted to ask Star questions about what had happened to the Library, but knew she should not, when listening devices could be all around.

Since Star had been invisible to Lucy, though, Lenora supposed Star could hide from anyone who wasn't a real librarian, including the Forces. Lenora wished greatly that she had this power. She resolved to return here and learn more, after matters with the Library were straightened out.

For now, Lenora decided it was best to stick with the topic at hand. "Star, I have a patron who is looking for the world's largest number. Can you tell me what it is?"

Surprisingly, a tremble rippled through Star, and Lenora sensed fear. "I can tell you many things about large numbers," said Star. "But that . . . I am afraid I cannot help you with. As a number myself, there are realms into which I dare not venture." And Star turned to face the deep darkness at the very far end of the hall. "Perhaps you and your friend could enter them, if you are brave."

Lenora worried about Lucy, for the girl had not sworn the librarian's oath to *venture forth bravely*, as Lenora had. But then she noticed Lucy was no longer clinging to her, and had in fact wandered over to the books on the long shelf. Perhaps she could adjust more quickly than it had seemed at first. Lenora went over to have a look.

Lucy pointed to the title of what was one of the thinnest books on the shelf. "Googol," she said, pronouncing the name on the cover. "What's that?"

Lenora turned the cover. Inside the book was only a single page of paper, and on it was nothing but a one followed by a very long string of zeros.

Star floated over. "A googol is simply one followed by a hundred zeros. A nine-year-old named Milton Sirotta invented the term."

Lenora already had her notebook out, and wrote quickly: *googol—word invented by ambitious nine-year-old.*

Star went on. "It is a rather famous and interesting number, but it is certainly not the longest, and has little use in mathematics. We keep it here only for historical interest." Star dipped to indicate another thin book nearby, titled *Avogadro's Number.* Lenora opened it to find a single page on which was written 602,214,150,000,000,000,000,000. "Avogadro's number," Star explained, "which is used to count up atoms and molecules for certain measurements, has a meaningful purpose in chemistry. That is what we mean by 'large numbers' in Googology. Numbers that mean something in the real world can be used to form equations and learn new truths, and can be counted up using one, two, three, four, and so on. And I suspect that is the very question your patron is asking. What is the largest number that has a meaning and purpose?"

Lenora looked down the long shelf, at books that were hundreds of feet high, and wondered what those books contained if they didn't contain the world's largest number.

She was just about to ask Star, when Lucy spoke up. "Oh great. More creeps."

Lenora whipped around. Three people were sliding down the slide.

No, not people, and not sliding, either. They were gliding, all three in a row, two men and one woman, all staring straight at Lenora. These were the Forces, and she was sure they were coming for her.

Star saw them, too. "I must hide. You two,

quickly, run. Run as far as you can, all the way to . . ." But Star's words faded as the ○ became only a shimmering once more. Lenora knew the Forces could not see it, but if Star spoke, they would know it was there. And so she grabbed Lucy's hand and tried to run.

But Lucy wouldn't move. "Don't be afraid, Lenora! Watch." She turned to the three Forces, who were nearly to the bottom of the slide. "You get out of here right now! You are scaring my friend."

The Forces did not stop. If anything, having now reached the bottom of the slide, they were gliding even faster, straight at the girls.

Lucy went very, very pale. "Run," Lenora said firmly, and this time Lucy ran.

The girls raced down the long, long shelf toward the deep darkness at its end. The Forces came on swiftly. Lenora risked a glance over her shoulder and saw they were gaining. Then she and Lucy came to a complete stop, for now they had reached a wall of darkness, covering the entire end of the room.

Both girls whipped around, their backs to the dark. And Lenora saw something strange. The Forces had stopped coming for them, and were now drifting back and forth, casting anxious glances up at the dark wall.

"They're scared of it," murmured Lenora in astonishment. She had never seen them show fear before. She could feel Lucy gripping her hand harder than ever.

Lenora could hear something now, something coming out of the dark. A whispering, a very far-away whispering, and then more and more, until there were dozens of whisperings coming from what seemed like an unimaginable distance.

The Forces appeared to have come to a decision, and resumed their advance toward Lenora and Lucy, slowly and deliberately this time. Lenora came to a decision, too. To escape these three, there was no other choice.

"Let's go," she said. Lucy nodded.

Hands clasped, they stepped backward into the dark.

CHAPTER EIGHT

Lenora and the Whispering Hoards

Lenora backed into the darkness and Lucy came with her. Once in, she found it was not completely dark—she could see Lucy faintly, as though by starlight. The distant whisperings could still be heard. Her heart pounding, she waited to see if the Forces would follow. They did not. Whatever was here, the Forces feared it. Lenora just hoped that anything the Forces feared meant nothing but good for her and Lucy.

"Uh, Lenora?" said Lucy. "What are we standing on?"

Lenora looked down. She had been right—almost— about the starlight. Faint points of light could be seen in all directions, up, down, and everywhere else. But they were not stars, for they did not twinkle. And they were not in space, where stars do not twinkle, because they could still breathe.

"I'm not sure," she admitted, for they seemed to be standing on nothing at all. She took a step, to see if they could walk. They could.

"What's that?" asked Lucy, pointing.

Lenora saw in the near distance what appeared to be a sign, lit from below by glowing lights. That made sense. This was still a library exhibition, after all, even if it was a very strange one, and things would have explanations somewhere. Toward the sign they went.

Soon they were standing in front of it, and both read silently:

I have this vision of hoards of shadowy numbers lurking out there in the dark, beyond the small sphere of light cast by the candle of reason. They are whispering to each other; plotting who knows what. Perhaps they don't like us very much for capturing their smaller brethren with our minds. Or perhaps they just live uniquely numberish lifestyles, out there beyond our ken.

—*Douglas Reay*

This sign was not at all helpful, but it sent a chill through Lenora. The whispering—were those hoards (she did not know why the word was *hoards* and not *hordes,* but somehow that made the message even more frightening) of shadowy numbers, plotting?

"Lenora," whispered Lucy, pressing close against her, "you were right about the creeps. Are they going to come after us?"

Lenora shook her head. "Not here, I don't think. The Forces of Darkness seem afraid of this place."

"Why do you call them the Forces of Darkness?" said Lucy. "That sounds evil."

"Lucy," said Lenora as gently as possible, "it's not something I invented. They have been known by that name for a very, very, very, very long time."

"Daddy must not know that!" exclaimed Lucy. "He can't possibly."

"I don't know," said Lenora. And that was true, for she had never met the Director and couldn't say. "Anyway, if they are afraid of this place, then they can't have fired anyone here."

And then she stopped, as she began to get the first glimmerings of an idea . . . if the Forces were afraid of this place, then maybe she could . . .

But her thoughts were interrupted when Lucy broke in. "So there must still be a librarian around here somewhere, right?"

"Oh, there is," said a voice, and once again Lenora and Lucy leapt about a foot in the air. And now she'd completely forgotten the idea she'd almost had. Lenora was getting rather tired of this, and felt that these invisible librarians really needed to cut it out.

But this librarian was not invisible. A small boy

stepped from behind the sign. He was fresh-faced and smiling, and dressed in very old-fashioned clothes. He had a librarian's badge, which read:

MILTON SIROTTA

⸻ ·⁚· ⸻

ONE GOOGOL

"You really didn't need to scare us like that," said Lenora crossly.

"I am deeply sorry," replied Milton in a soft voice. "I sensed the Forces were near, and even though they are afraid to enter this section, I thought it best to hide nevertheless."

"What exactly are they scared of, anyway?" asked Lucy.

"There are beings here that they cannot understand or control. And that frightens them more than anything else, as it should. They could destroy all books of history, and history would be lost to us forever. They could destroy all poetry, and that would be lost forever, too. But these beings—the numbers, math itself—even if you destroyed all books of math, it could be rediscovered. So here is something the Forces of Darkness are powerless against."

That sounded to Lenora as though she and Lucy had nothing to fear, either, and Milton himself was utterly at ease—but she was determined to keep her guard up regardless. Of the many unexpected dilemmas she'd faced in the Library, this was one of the most unsettling. She needed more information. "Are you really Milton Sirotta?" she asked.

The boy shook his head. "No, not really. I am a googol, which is—"

"One followed by a hundred zeros," interrupted Lucy. "We know."

"Ah," replied the boy. "Well, then you also know that I was named by nine-year-old Milton Sirotta. And so, for purposes of helping anyone who might enter this section (very few do), I have chosen to take on his form. You may address me as Milton, which I rather prefer to 'Googol.'"

"I can relate," said Lucy sympathetically. "I hate my real name, too."

"All right, Milton," said Lenora, a bit impatiently. "I need to know what the world's largest number is."

"Hmm," said Milton. "That really depends on a number of factors. And *they* have their own opinions, of course."

"They?" said Lenora.

"Yes," said Milton. "Can't you hear them?"

"The whispering," said Lenora, whispering, too. Shadowy numbers whispering things she could not understand—she did not like this at all.

"Correct. They live out there, far off in the dark, at distances one can scarcely imagine."

"What are they whispering about?"

"I'm not always sure," said Milton. "I'm unsure most of the time, really."

"But aren't you a large number?" asked Lenora.

"Oh, yes. Very large. In fact, the total number of electrons, protons, and neutrons in the entire observable universe is less than me." Lenora began scribbling furiously in her notebook. "Quite a lot less, in fact. But that's really nothing. Milton also invented the term *googolplex,* which is one followed by a googol zeros. Next to that, I am nothing. If you wrote one digit of a googolplex on every Planck volume in the universe—"

"A Planck volume is basically the smallest thing that isn't nothing," Lenora explained to Lucy, who had just opened her mouth to ask.

"—you would run out of space long before you finished writing the number. It simply can't be done. Even if you use regular English to write the number's actual name, it's ten tremilliatrecentretriginmilliatrecentretriginmilliatrecentretriginmilliamilliamilliamil-

liamilliamilliamilliamilliamilliamilliamilliamil-
liamilliamilliamilliamilliamilliamilliamilliamil-
liamilliamilliamilliamilliamilliamilliamilliamil-
liamilliamilliatrecentretriginmilliamilliamilliamil-
liamilliamilliamilliamilliamilliamilliamilliamil-
liamilliamilliamilliamilliamilliamilliamilliamil-
liamilliamilliamilliamilliamilliamilliamilliamil-
liamilliatrecentretriginmilliamilliamilliamilliamil-
liamilliamilliamilliamilliamilliamilliamilliamil-
liamilliamilliamilliamilliamilliamilliamilliamil-
liamilliamilliamilliamilliamilliamilliatrecen-
tretriginmilliamilliamilliamilliamilliamilliamil-
liamilliamilliamilliamilliamilliamilliamilliamil-
liamilliamilliamilliamilliamilliamilliamilliamil-
liamilliamilliamilliatrecentretriginmilliamil-
liamilliamilliamilliamilliamilliamilliamilliamil-
liamilliamilliamilliamilliamilliamilliamilliamil-
liamilliamilliamilliamilliamilliamilliamilliamil-
liatrecentretriginmilliamilliamilliamilliamil-
liamilliamilliamilliamilliamilliamilliamilliamil-
liamilliamilliamilliamilliamilliamilliamilliamil-
liamilliamilliatrecentretriginmilliamilliamil-
liamilliamilliamilliamilliamilliamilliamilliamil-

liamilliamilliamilliamilliamilliamilliamilliamil-
liamilliamilliamilliamilliamilliatrecentretriginmil-
liamilliamilliamilliamilliamilliamilliamilliamil-
liamilliamilliamilliamilliamilliamilliamilliamil-
liamilliamilliamilliamilliamilliatrecentre-
triginmilliamilliamilliamilliamilliamilliamilliamil-
liamilliamilliamilliamilliamilliamilliamilliamil-
liamilliamilliamilliamilliamilliatrecentre-
triginmilliamilliamilliamilliamilliamilliamilliamil-
liamilliamilliamilliamilliamilliamilliamilliamil-
liamilliamilliamilliamilliatrecentretriginmil-
liamilliamilliamilliamilliamilliamilliamilliamil-
liamilliamilliamilliamilliamilliamilliamilliamil-
liamilliamilliamilliatrecentretriginmilliamilliamil-
liamilliamilliamilliamilliamilliamilliamilliamilli-
amilliamilliamilliamilliamilliamilliamilliatre-
centretriginmilliamilliamilliamilliamilliamilliamil-
liamilliamilliamilliamilliamilliamilliamilliamilli-
amilliamilliatrecentretriginmilliamilliamil-
liamilliamilliamilliamilliamilliamilliamilliamil-
liamilliamilliamilliamilliamilliamilliatrecentre-
triginmilliamilliamilliamilliamilliamilliamilliamil-
liamilliamilliamilliamilliamilliamilliamilliamil-

liatrecentretriginmilliamilliamilliamilliamilliamil-
liamilliamilliamilliamilliamilliamilliamilliamil-
liamilliatrecentretriginmilliamilliamilliamilliamil-
liamilliamilliamilliamilliamilliamilliamilliamil-
liamilliatrecentretriginmilliamilliamilliamilliamil-
liamilliamilliamilliamilliamilliamilliamilliamil-
liatrecentretriginmilliamilliamilliamilliamilliamil-
liamilliamilliamilliamilliamilliatrecentretrig-
inmilliamilliamilliamilliamilliamilliamilliamilli-
amilliamilliamilliatrecentretriginmilliamilliamil-
liamilliamilliamilliamilliamilliamilliamilliatrecen-
tretriginmilliamilliamilliamilliamilliamilliamilli-
amilliamilliatrecentretriginmilliamilliamilliamil-
liamilliamilliamilliamilliatrecentretriginmilliamil-
liamilliamilliamilliamilliamilliatrecentretriginmil-
liamilliamilliamilliamilliamilliatrecentretriginmil-
liamilliamilliamilliamilliatrecentretriginmilliamil-
liamilliamilliatrecentretriginmilliamilliamilliatre-
centretriginmilliamilliatrecentretriginmilliatrecen-
duotrigintillion. So you can see it's rather long no
matter how you look at it."

At the beginning, Lenora had tried to write that
down, but had quickly given up as Milton went

along. "So a googolplex is the largest number?" she asked.

"Oh, no," laughed Milton. "Not even close."

"Well then, what is it?"

Milton said. "I don't know. As I said, the great numbers are far beyond me."

Lenora's head was spinning at the thought of all this, but Lucy had her chin in her hand, deep in thought. "Why don't we just go talk to them, then? They could tell us."

"*Talk* to them?" said Lenora and Milton together. Lenora wasn't sure about this, and Milton looked alarmed as well. These large numbers were sounding more dangerous all the time. Lenora wondered if the Forces of Darkness hadn't been right to stay away. Still, she had no choice but to get an answer for her patron. She'd already let one patron down on Plato's *Republic*, and she didn't plan on that happening again. "Good idea, Lucy. Let's do it. Is that all right with you, Milton? Can you take us to them?"

Milton looked uncertain, but he nodded. "I can. But you must proceed carefully. You are to the great numbers as a top quark is to you."

"A top what?" said Lucy.

Lenora was very glad she had read *Your Friends, the Subatomic Particles* over the summer. "A top quark is an extremely tiny particle that lives for less than a trillionth of a trillionth of a second."

"Yes," said Milton. "And to the large numbers, you are little different from that. So to meet them, we must get large ourselves. Very large indeed. Give me your hands."

They did. And then they grew—very, very, very, very large indeed.

CHAPTER NINE
Lenora and the Numbers

Lenora had once seen the glory of the stars from outer space when she had been tossed through the open door of a rocket ship. She recognized them again, but saw them so briefly it hardly counted, before she was staring down at a double-armed disc of stars disappearing beneath her feet—the Milky Way galaxy, dwindling to a speck. Around her, Lucy, and Milton were clusters of other galaxies, which in turn became smaller blurs of light until they couldn't be seen at all.

Lenora could scarcely believe it, but she, Lucy,

and Milton were zooming up, larger and larger, the trillions of galaxies streaking past like shooting stars, and then they were beyond even those, and now below her Lenora could see one collection of lights, all the universe in something like a bubble, but . . . different. She thought, but couldn't be sure, that there were other bubblish things nearby, but her mind was too rattled to be sure of any of it. And then all that vanished away into nothing, also.

Lenora looked over at Lucy, whose eyes and mouth were wide with wonder. It seemed she, too, could understand what had happened, that they were larger, far larger now, than the universe, or perhaps many universes. Lenora's brain trembled at the thought.

"Here we are," said Milton. "This is where the large numbers live." He was perfectly calm, though Lenora was on the verge of telling him to take them back to normal size. For something in her bones told her: *Humans are not supposed to be here.*

She held her tongue. Lucy looked thrilled,

Milton probably did this all the time, and Lenora had a patron who needed an answer. She did want to get this over with as quickly as possible, though, and so she asked, "What now?"

Milton thought for a moment. "Let's meet Graham's number. He might be willing to speak with us. Not all of them are." And then, though she could not tell how, they began moving, flying really, toward one of the lights that still surrounded them.

As they flew, Lenora remembered the third task Malachi had given her. And so she asked, "By the way—do you know who Zenodotus is?"

"Of course!" said Milton. "He was the first head librarian of the Library of Alexandria."

"Oh!" said Lenora.

"What's that?" said Lucy.

"It was considered the greatest library of the ancient world, founded in Egypt long ago," said Lenora. And then, to Milton: "Do you know where Zenodotus is? I have to find him."

"No," said Milton, "I have not seem him in

quite some time. But I remember him as a dashing man with a long, curled mustache, full of energy and life."

Lucy spoke up. "Wouldn't it be easy to find him? Let's just go to this Library of Alex-whatever-ia and see if he's there."

"It's not there anymore," said Milton. "I'm not sure what happened, but I heard it was accidentally burned down in 48 BC by Julius Caesar."

"What a dummy," said Lucy.

Lenora scribbled *L of A destroyed by Caesar's fire—maybe* in her notebook. Then she saw they were coming swiftly toward one of the lights, and soon Lenora could make out a man sitting on a chair amid a brilliant gleam. He wore a flat-brimmed straw hat and an elegant old striped suit. He sat with one leg crossed over the other and took no notice of them at all. He seemed deep in thought, and though his lips did not move, Lenora could hear a whispering coming from him.

The three stopped in front of the man, and Milton bowed low. Lenora and Lucy looked at each other, and then Lenora bowed deeply, too, while Lucy executed an elegant curtsy.

"Sir," said Milton, "may we please speak with you for a moment? This librarian has a question."

The man did not respond, still gazing at something faraway, still whispering.

Lenora whispered, too. "Who is this?"

Milton spoke low, as though he did not want to disturb the man. "This is Graham's number. He is the result of certain calculations concerning the edges of many-dimensional cubes. He was once the largest number ever produced by a mathematical proof. But that record has since been broken."

At this, the man's head turned slowly toward them, and Milton immediately went silent. Graham's number regarded each of them in turn for what seemed to Lenora like a terribly long time. First Lucy, then Lenora, and then his gaze, which was not a friendly one, landed on Milton.

"Why have you disturbed me?" he asked in a soft voice with just a hint of menace. "I am engaged in several very important conversations."

"I apologize, sir," said Milton, bowing again. "But this librarian is searching for the largest number. I thought you might be able to direct us."

The man uncrossed his legs and looked hard at them. "Am I not large enough for you? What use could you possibly have for anyone larger?"

Lenora spoke up. "Sir, if I may ask—how large are you, exactly?"

Graham's number looked at her, and his gaze softened slightly. "A librarian. I would like to tell you how large I am. However, there is nothing your mind can understand, nothing I can be compared to, that will aid you in understanding my vast size. I am far beyond the realm of your imagination."

Lenora wondered how bold she dared be. "Thank you, sir." And then she hesitated before saying, "Milton has told us there are larger numbers than even you. Perhaps you can tell me the largest of you?" She hoped this would not offend.

Graham's number turned his gaze back to whatever he had been doing before. "Ask TREE(3), if it will speak to you. It is the next number that humans—you are human, are you not?—were able to discover beyond me." And then he went back to his whispering. Lenora had a feeling he would not speak to them again.

The three silently withdrew, Milton still holding both girls' hands. Lenora sensed hesitation from the boy. "Is something wrong?" she asked.

"It's TREE(3)," replied Milton with a tremor in his voice. "I have never encountered it before. But I have heard it is not friendly, not friendly at all. Perhaps we should stop here."

Lenora was worried, but firm. "I must have an answer for my patron. If you will not go on, please show me how to go myself, and you and Lucy can go back and wait for me."

"No way!" announced Lucy, who, against all odds, seemed to be having the time of her life. "I'm going with Lenora!"

"Very well," said Milton. "It is better that I go with you, then. A mere googol may or may not be beneath notice in this realm, but two humans certainly will. No offense meant."

"None taken," said Lenora.

The children squeezed each other's hands tightly

as they flew off again, this time toward a brilliant light farther above. As they went, Milton said, "I might as well tell you that TREE(3) is just a way of counting up 'trees' you can draw like this." He released Lenora's hand long enough to borrow her notebook.

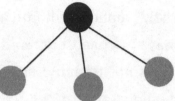

He continued, "They're drawn according to certain rules. It's quite a bit simpler to understand than Graham's number, but . . . well, we shall see what TREE(3) has to say."

Now they were nearing something absolutely enormous—Lenora was not surprised to see it was a tree, but of such massive size that its branches extended in all directions farther than the eye could see, and the light that poured from it was nearly blinding. The three of them were as small before it as a tardigrade would be in front of Devils Tower. It reminded Lenora of what she had read of

Yggdrasil, the world tree of Norse mythology that connects nine different worlds.

She had plenty of time to ponder this connection, because TREE(3) did not react to them in any way whatsoever, no matter how many bows and curtsies and polite entreaties they produced. But Lenora was not about to give up (how could she possibly fail two patrons in a row?). She decided she'd had enough bowing and curtsying and begging. She was a librarian, after all, and she would not be ignored.

She walked up to TREE(3) and raised a fist.

"Uh . . ." said Milton.

Lenora gave TREE(3) a firm knock. "Hello? Hey? Listen to us. I've got a question I have to answer!"

"Lenora, I—" said Milton, backing away and pulling Lucy with him.

"Lemme go," cried Lucy, pulling back. "I wanna help Lenora!"

Lenora knocked again. "Hello?!"

TREE(3) began to shake. First, the smallest vibration. Then, its branches began to shake. Then, a mighty tremor shook the air, and TREE(3) came to life, roaring, "YOU DARE?"

And then the mighty branches closed around them, coming together as though to squash them all flat.

CHAPTER TEN
Lenora and the TREEs

A voice spoke. "Oh, stop it."

The voice was the smallest and squeakiest Lenora could imagine, but for some reason, TREE(3) returned immediately to its immense, remote silence.

"Hello," said the voice. "Down here."

Everyone looked down. Sitting at the base of the enormous tree was a much smaller tree, something that looked to Lenora like a bonsai-sized version of TREE(3), which you could put in your backpack.

"Thank you," said Lenora with immense relief. "May I ask who you are?"

"I am TREE(2). It's very nice to meet you."

This TREE was certainly nicer than the other, and Lenora felt that they ought to shake hands or something, but of course they had no way of doing that. So she simply asked, politely, "Are you a large number as well?"

TREE(2) laughed. (Lenora was not exactly sure where its voice was coming from.) "No, not at all. You see, TREEs grow quickly. TREE(1), for example, is only equal to one. And I, TREE(2), am only equal to three. TREE(3), on the other hand, is a number so incomprehensibly vast that it defies any description I could give you. There is no written notation that can express it. TREE(3) makes Graham's number (I believe you've met) look like nothing in comparison."

"So it's the largest number, then?" asked Lenora hopefully.

"Oh, no," said TREE(2). "Of course, they thought that for a while. But then someone found one larger. Every so often, a new one is discovered. It's all quite exciting, at least to us."

"Well, thank you," said Lenora. She did not want to seem ungrateful, but how on earth would she give that boy his answer? Then again, the idea that one could keep discovering ever-larger numbers was rather thrilling. But given what she had seen from TREE(3), Lenora wasn't so sure she wanted to meet any more of them.

Nevertheless, she turned to Milton. "I suppose we should keep going."

A voice spoke from behind them. "No. You shouldn't."

Lenora whirled around. "Malachi! How did you get here?"

Malachi looked down at the three of them, and Lucy gaped up at the astonishing sight of the ten-foot-tall Assistant Answerer. (Though Lenora wondered why she still seemed ten feet tall when all of them were larger than the observable universe at the moment.)

Lucy looked down at her own platform shoes,

then up at Malachi. "How did you get to be so tall?" she demanded.

"A stretching machine," replied Malachi gravely. "I use it every day."

"Really?" asked Lucy.

"No," said Malachi, and turned to Lenora. "Lenora, I must be brief. You should know that I am being watched at all times. There are few places in the Library I can speak freely, and this is one of them. As you know, the Forces fear this place, and they cannot spy on us here."

"But why haven't they just fired you?" asked Lenora, hard as it was to imagine anyone throwing Malachi out of the Library.

Malachi closed her eyes and took a deep breath. "Only the Director can give orders such as firing a librarian—"

"Daddy would *never* do that!" Lucy interrupted.

"—and so I made the decision, and I hope it was the correct one, to give the appearance of cooperation with him. I wish to fight from within, though I am still not fully trusted. But we have no further time to discuss this. The Director has been informed of your presence and that you are with his daughter, and he ordered the Forces to find you immediately. They are on their way here despite their fears, and so you must go."

"I'm not going anywhere," said Lenora. "I still don't have an answer for my patron."

"Are you certain of that? Perhaps you have an answer, though not the one you were seeking."

Lenora knew better than to ask Malachi what that answer was. She expected to be told it would be best to figure it out for herself, of course. And so she would. In the meantime . . .

"Where can we go?" asked Lenora. "If we can't hide from the Director here, then where can we?"

"We're not hiding from Daddy, are we?" ventured Lucy plaintively. "Just those creepy Forces people, right?"

Malachi was frowning. "Hide?" she said. "Hiding is hardly in your nature, Lenora. Now, where would the Director be least likely to expect you?"

Lenora thought of her oath. *Think on my feet and rely on my wits and valor . . .*

She turned to the others. "I know where we're going. We're going to the Director."

"Yay!" cheered Lucy.

"What?" cried Milton, aghast.

"Correct," replied Malachi. "Now go to him before the Forces catch up. I have every confidence in you." She looked at Milton. "Show them the way immediately. I must go."

"Yes, ma'am," said Milton. And then Malachi was gone.

In an instant they were shrinking, shrinking at an impossibly fast rate as the universe and galaxies and stars all rushed by, this time getting larger instead of smaller.

And then they were standing in front of the sign again, Lenora fuming all the while. How had she gotten an answer for her patron? She didn't see it. But this was not the time to figure it out, and so she asked Milton, "How can we get out of here if the Forces are coming?" For there had not seemed to be a way back up that slide, even if the room beyond the dark wall were not already filled with enemies.

As she pondered this, the glimmering idea

returned. Lenora snapped her fingers. "Milton, if the Forces are afraid to come here, could librarians use this as sort of a hideout, like a . . . a . . ."

"A rebel base!" said Lucy. "Cool."

"Exactly," replied Lenora with a smile.

"Certainly," said Milton. "We do have plenty of room, after all. But in the meantime, you should go." He waved his hand. Instantly, a single tube capsule appeared, seemingly suspended in the darkness. "This is my personal capsule. You can take it straight to the Director. And . . . good luck." He did not look especially confident.

Lenora did not blame him. She herself was, frankly, quite alarmed. Lucy, however, was simply giddy. "Yes, let's go see Daddy! I can't wait for him to meet you, Lenora! I'm sure he will get those Forces creeps straightened out."

And so the girls climbed in, and Lenora saw something new—a large, brilliantly glowing label, twice the size of any other, that said in bright letters: DIRECTOR.

Steeling herself, Lenora inserted her key, and they were off.

After a speedy journey, the tube slowed and stopped. The door popped open.

Lenora got out, followed by Lucy. In front of them was a short set of stairs that seemed to be made of, or at least coated in, pure platinum, a silvery sort of extremely valuable metal that Lenora had learned all about in *Metallurgy: From Aluminum to Zirconium and Back Again*. At the top of the steps were some rather over-decorated doors, and above that the words THE DIRECTOR, also in platinum, and above that a gigantic portrait of the Director, which made him look quite a lot younger and even handsomer than he was. That was framed in platinum, too. Lenora rather thought you could overdo it with the platinum, but then the doors burst open and everything changed.

Several members of the Forces, disguised, of course, as librarians, came rushing down the steps. But the expressions on their faces were unlike anything Lenora had seen from them before. They were unsure, rather pale, surprised, and they were saying things to one another like:

"—what did she—?"

"—why? Where did they—?"

"—where is—but how—?"

Lenora couldn't make it all out because they were babbling over one another. But this was exactly what Lenora had been hoping for. The Forces had expected her to run or hide, but instead she had come straight at them, taking them completely by surprise, and they had no idea what she was doing or why, and perhaps—just perhaps—were a little afraid that she might have some kind of plan.

She did not, of course, have a plan. But she did realize, for this moment at least, that she had an advantage and must make use of it immediately. So she grabbed Lucy's hand and said, "Let's go see your daddy!" in the brightest and most confident voice she could possibly muster.

"Yes!" said Lucy, enthused, and up the stairs they dashed, right past all the Forces. A couple of them moved as though to block them, then hesitated, and before any decision could be made Lenora and Lucy were through the door.

And there was the Director.

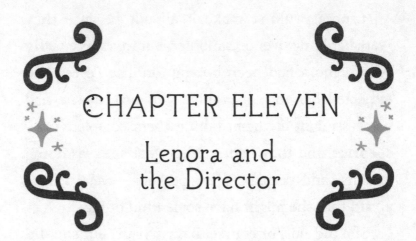

CHAPTER ELEVEN

Lenora and the Director

He was sitting behind a huge mahogany desk with nothing on it, a desk set up on a dais so that Lenora had to crane her neck to look up at him. He was the same handsome man with salt-and-pepper hair that Lenora had seen in the videos, but he was not smiling or speaking, just staring down at Lenora with his lips tightly pursed into a petulant scowl, as though she had spilled something on the thick, red, expensive-looking carpet. On his chest was a huge platinum badge that read THE DIRECTOR. The walls were decorated with many portraits of a younger and even more handsome version of the man.

The only other thing in the room was a machine along one wall covered with monitors and dials and switches and microphones. There was a sign above it that said TRANSMISSION CONSOLE.

Lucy, for her part, screeched, "Daddyyyyyyyyyy!" then rushed up the dais and threw herself into his lap. The pursed scowl vanished, and the Director said, "Princess!" while giving her a hug. From behind Lenora, all the Forces rushed up to the dais and placed themselves in a semicircular arrangement behind the Director. It felt vaguely protective and a little threatening at the same time.

The Director released Lucy and resumed scowling at Lenora. "So you caught her," he announced. "I told you it would be easy if you stopped being such cowards."

"They didn't catch—" Lenora began, thoroughly outraged, but was spoken over by several of the Forces:

"Yes, sir, you were absolutely right as always, sir—"

"Of course, we just thought about you, and how bravely you would handle it yourself—"

"Without you we never could have—"

The Director leaned back in his chair, beaming and basking in all this praise, smiling and tousling the hair of Lucy, who gazed up at him adoringly.

Lenora had an idea.

"That's right, sir!" she yelled over the din. "They did a fantastic job catching me. I don't think anyone's plan could have worked better than yours! And now here I am."

One of the women behind the Director was staring daggers at her. Lenora stared them right back.

Now the Director looked puzzled. He turned to one of the Forces. "You told me the girl who had taken my Princess was very rude and not respectful. But she seems very intelligent. Are you sure this is the right one? The enemy?"

Lucy broke in before anyone could answer. "Lenora's not the enemy! She took me to a huge slide and it was so much fun, and then we met a googol and grew bigger than the whole universe and met more numbers and then there was this *really* tall woman"—every single member of the Forces jumped at *that* news—"and—"

"That's nice, Princess," said the Director, patting her on the head. "You have such a good, good imagination. Almost as good as mine, which is the best, isn't it?" He turned expectantly toward the Forces, and they said, "Oh yes, sir! It's a great, great imagination. The greatest ever." But none of them looked very happy. Not at all.

One of them continued, "But you see, sir—as you know, libraries can be very dangerous. And allowing Princess to run around with this girl who keeps finding herself in bad situations—well, sir, Princess could get hurt, you see. Or even worse."

The Director sighed. "I suppose you are right. We must look out for Princess."

"But Daddy!" Lucy pouted. "I learned so much from Lenora. Did you know that people used to work computers by hand? And that—"

"Now, now, Princess," her father interrupted. "You know that if you want to learn anything, you don't need to read any books or ask any silly librarians. You can just ask me! I know everything."

And for the first time, Lenora could see just the smallest bit of doubt creep over Lucy's face, even though she still seemed to love the hair tousling. (Lenora wondered how she could possibly stand five seconds of it.)

Lenora grasped the opportunity. "That's true, sir. The Philosophy section, for example. I love what you've done with it. All of those great . . . great . . . books, all written by you. What else could anyone need?"

"That's exactly what *I* said," the Director replied. "Didn't I?" He looked around, and the Forces nodded with extraordinary reluctance.

Lenora felt she was really getting the hang of this. "Yes, all those old, really, really famous philosophers, stretching back thousands of years. You always knew someone was great when you saw their name alongside great, big philosophers, like Plato and Aristotle and those other famous Greek guys. Even though we don't really *need* them anymore."

"That's right," mused the Director, who seemed to be struggling with something. A thought, perhaps.

Lenora waited. The Forces were all looking on in extreme alarm.

The Director snapped his fingers. "You know, I just had another great idea. We should put all those old philosopher guys back up. It will make me look even better, and no one is going to read their dumb books anyway when they can read mine."

"What a *great* idea," said Lenora.

"But sir!" said one of the Forces in horror. "The Board has directly ordered——"

The Director waved his hand absently. "The Board, the Board, the Board. You know what? *I'm* bored." He paused to laugh uproariously at his own joke, then continued, "The Board, look, they work for me, okay? They do what I say. I'm the Director."

"The Board does *not* work——" began one of the Forces, then stopped as he saw all the rest of them shaking their heads wildly.

The Director began to get red-faced, then quickly became purple-faced. The veins on his neck bulged. Lenora got the distinct impression the man was about to lose his temper quite dramatically. "What did you say?"

"Never mind him. It's a great decision, sir," said a woman soothingly. "He just means that we will have to inform the Board, of course. It's merely standard policy."

"Fine," fumed the Director. "Tell them. Make sure they know who's boss around here."

"Of course," said the woman, casting a triumphant look at Lenora.

Lenora began to get a rather worse feeling about the Board than she'd even had before, and she was not as confident as the Director that he was quite as much in control of them as he seemed to think.

"Good," said the Director. "Now get down to Philosophy and put all those old guys back up. And mix them around a bunch so they're always next to my books."

The librarian in Lenora shuddered at this lack of order. But at least the books would be back on the shelves. And then she was extremely surprised at what the Director said next.

"And *she's* in charge of it," he said, pointing at Lenora. "I like her. You guys leave her alone. She's cooperating."

Several of the Forces hissed at these words.

"Can I go with her, Daddy?" cried Lucy. "Lenora is so much fun."

"Anything for my Princess!" said the Director, and Lucy leapt from his lap and ran to Lenora, who turned to leave. She could feel the Forces gathering behind her, ready to follow.

"And I'm going to make an announcement to the Philosophy section about my great idea!" said the Director, walking over to the transmission console. "Message to Philosophy," he began. "No," he said. "The whole Library should know about this. It's genius." He flipped another switch from Off to Live and went straight into one of his speeches, his face appearing on every monitor, happy as could be.

"Hello, patrons!" he exclaimed, face abeam. "As you know, I have been removing many unnecessary and expensive books in order to make the Library a more exciting and entertaining experience for all of you!"

Lenora felt her left eye begin to twitch.

"And of course my policy has been incredibly successful and is making you all much smarter. But

I have decided to bring back a few of those books, by some of those famous Greek guys, like uh . . . uh . . . ."

The agonizing pause continued until Lenora whispered, "Plato and Aristotle!"

"Uh, yes, Platotle and all the rest . . ."

Lenora couldn't take it anymore. She went straight down the steps to the Tube, the Forces following, as the Director continued blathering away in the background.

There was a man ascending the steps. A man wearing a green raincoat. And he was smiling serenely at Lenora as he ascended.

Goose bumps rose on her arms.

Lenora felt hate surge inside her, hate she had never felt before. Her blood was pounding in her veins, and her breaths were coming faster and faster. By the time the man in the green raincoat was next to her on the steps, still smiling at her pleasantly, she wanted nothing more in the world than to hurl herself at him, hitting him with her fists, and then to do the same to every single one of the Forces following her. A kind of red blindness came over her, and, fists curled, she threw herself at him—

Or would have, had arms not wrapped around her from behind. "Lenora!" Lucy was shouting. "What's wrong? Lenora, stop!"

Lenora fought, pulling at Lucy's arms, wanting to fight Lucy, too, even though the deepest part of her brain was telling her *stop you don't want this stop stop stop* . . .

And then the man in the green raincoat leaned down and whispered in Lenora's ear, so softly that even Lucy could not hear, a whisper that slithered and writhed like a cobra about to strike, a voice that was not at all human: *You won, little girl. But only for a moment. There are thousands of us everywhere here, and soon enough we will eat you and that giantess and everything else, and burn this Library to the ground just like we did the others.*

And then there were several popping sounds. The man and the rest of the Forces vanished.

Lenora sagged in Lucy's arms, her desire to fight gone. She felt only a deep weariness, like a sickness had passed through her. Lucy released her, and Lenora slumped onto the steps.

"Lenora, what happened?" cried Lucy, sounding almost in tears. "Are you okay?"

"I'm . . . sorry," Lenora said, hardly able to muster words. "I . . . don't know. It was . . . was like . . . like I wasn't myself."

"Maybe we should go back and ask Daddy," Lucy said anxiously. "You might be sick."

"No," said Lenora. Her strength was coming back to her, but slowly. "We must keep on. Just— help me into the tube."

With one arm around Lucy for support, Lenora climbed into the tube and fell into the seat. With Lucy beside her, she inserted her key with a shaking hand and set them on their way to Philosophy.

CHAPTER TWELVE
Lenora and Flight

O nce they reached the Philosophy section,
Lenora was feeling much better, and though
quite worried about the episode with the man in
the green raincoat, she still had a job to do. And so
she did it.

Lenora certainly felt odd giving orders to the
Forces of Darkness, who were only disguised as
humans, and who certainly had no desire to take any
orders from her. But take her orders they did, as
they brought in boxes and boxes of books that had
been hidden away in some other location (Lenora

was determined to find out where) and began to put the books back on the Philosophy section's shelves.

All the boxes were marked FOR IMMEDIATE DISPOSAL. Lenora sighed in relief as each box emptied.

She did her best to direct the Forces to put the books in the correct location, while still sticking with the Director's command that they be mixed in with his. While she was at it, she decided to see how far, exactly, this new cooperation would go.

"So," Lenora said casually to one of the Forces, this one taking on the appearance of an elderly woman (Lenora felt that she might have seen this one before, but she couldn't remember where), who was bitterly shelving Thomas Hobbes's *Leviathan* next to the Director's *How to Be Almost as Good-Looking as Me*. "Why are you taking orders from the Director, anyway? You and I both know you're really just an evil monster."

The woman merely hissed in reply. Lenora failed to flinch, having gotten used to these hisses, and turned away, realizing that she perhaps might have been more diplomatic. But the Forces seemed unlikely to answer her queries anyway.

Lucy trailed after Lenora as she moved down the shelves, making sure the Forces weren't cheating by leaving any books in the boxes. "So they're really evil monsters, huh?" she whispered to Lenora. "How can you tell?"

"I don't know," Lenora said. "I just can."

Lucy stayed very close to Lenora after that.

At last the work was done, and the very moment the final book went onto a shelf, all the Forces gave Lenora one last murderous look (they'd been giving them to her the entire time, which, like the hisses, had become boring rather quickly, so Lenora hardly noticed), then popped into nothing, off to wherever they went when they did that.

"Finally," said Lucy. "Now let's do something fun!"

"I have a job to do, Lucy," said Lenora. "And I'm going to do it. But I am pretty sure that if you come along you'll find out this job provides more fun than you can handle."

"Okay!" said Lucy, hopping in place, ready to go. "And we can go wherever we want now, because Daddy told those Forces to leave you alone. They won't come after you anymore."

Lenora thought for a moment. "And do you still think your father knows everything, Lucy?"

Lucy paused. "Well, he thought I was making all that stuff up about the slide rules and big numbers and stuff, so . . . maybe he doesn't know *every*thing. But he's really smart."

Lenora decided to leave it at that for now. She took one last look around Philosophy, feeling deep satisfaction. She had managed to restore one section, at least. But doubt quickly crept in. She was only one librarian, and the Library overall was in terrible shape. How could she possibly save it all, when even a librarian as powerful as Malachi had been rendered almost helpless?

She shook herself. *One step at a time, Lenora,* she thought. *That's the only way any big job ever gets done.* And then she said to Lucy, "Let's go."

Before they left, Lenora plucked one copy of Plato's *Republic* off a shelf and dropped it into her pocket. If she once again ran into the woman who'd bought an island, she wanted to make sure she had a copy.

The pair walked out of Philosophy. Lenora looked up and down the impossibly long hallway outside. She shivered a little at the eerie sight. Normally, these hallways were bustling with librarians and patrons and who knew what else. But now they were largely empty, with only a few confused-looking patrons wandering around, no doubt trying to find a librarian to help them. Lenora wondered how many real librarians were left.

Then she spotted one. A librarian whose badge said PHILLIP went rushing past, and he had a box in his hands and tears on his cheeks. Lenora knew exactly what this meant, and she leapt to intercept him. "Wait! Don't leave!" she cried, grasping his elbow.

Phillip looked at her. "I have to," he said in a broken voice. "I've been fired."

Lenora thought fast. Motioning to him to lean down, she cupped her hands around her mouth and whispered in his ear, "Go to Googology. The

Forces are frightened of the large numbers. You'll be safe there." And then she had another, even better thought. "And find Aaliyah and Paolo and take them with you. And spread the word to every real librarian: We've got a rebel base."

Phillip straightened and looked at Lenora, eyes wide. "Lenora," he said, "everything they've said about you is true. Thank you."

Everything they've said about me? thought Lenora. *What did* that *mean?*

Phillip moved to leave, but Lenora said, "Wait!" and motioned again. He leaned down. "Do you know where I can find Zenodotus?"

"No," whispered Phillip. "I've never even met him. But I've heard he is always rushing around the Library in his blue robe, full of vigor and strength. It's amazing how he could go on after the Library of Alexandria was destroyed in AD 272 by the armies of the emperor Aurelian. Or at least, that's what I heard." Then he turned around and ran back in the direction he'd come.

Lenora was becoming more and more impressed by this Zenodotus. He sounded like exactly the man who could save the Library. Lenora was also becoming less and less impressed that no one seemed to really know how the Library of Alexandria had come to an end. In her notebook, she added, *No one seems to know true L of A story. Find out.*

Then Lucy was tugging on her arm. "Lenora! Look!" She pointed across the hallway, where a koala wearing a green backpack was scampering by.

Lenora got a creeping feeling as she watched the koala go. "Something is off about that koala."

"What's wrong?" asked Lucy as it slipped out of sight. "Is it one of the Forces?"

Lenora shook her head. "No, but . . ."

They were interrupted by a voice. "Excuse me, are you a librarian?"

They turned. Before them was a confused-looking boy about Lenora's age. He had black hair and olive skin and was holding a wrench in one hand and a screwdriver in the other.

"Yes, I'm a librarian," said Lenora. "Hello. How may I help you?"

"At last!" said the boy, rubbing the back of his head and blushing faintly as he looked at Lenora.

"A librarian! I have been looking everywhere for one. I need help with the contest. I'm so close!" He pointed at a sign next to an archway:

GLIDER BUILDING CONTEST

THIS WEEK ONLY!

Lenora looked up to see the name of the section, which said simply: FLIGHT.

"I really need help with my school project," the boy said. "My glider's all messed up. It's really terrible. I've done an awful job."

"We'll see about that!" said Lenora. "Lead me to your project . . ."

"Haruto," said Haruto, and off they went into Flight, Lucy tagging along eagerly.

The section was huge, as Lenora supposed it had to be. Hanging from the ceiling were all sorts of flying machines, like hot-air balloons (Lenora shuddered), airplanes, dirigibles, autogyros, and even a rather eye-catching red kite, which seemed to be flying in circles all by itself.

Getting to the glider contest area was difficult.

The three had to clamber up several ladders and through a few trapdoors as they ascended to the heights of Flight. Lenora wondered if the Forces of Darkness simply hadn't managed to get up here yet. At last they reached a long row of work areas, the floor of the section far below them. People were working busily at various gliders. Lenora was doubtful about a few of them, having had a bit of experience with flying. Finally the three passed by one particularly impressive project. It was a sleek, beautiful machine, which looked all the world like a finished glider as far as Lenora could tell.

But Lenora didn't praise this glider, as Haruto was so insecure about his own. "So where is your project, Haruto?"

Haruto blushed even harder. "This is it," he said.

Lenora cocked her head. "Haruto, this is amazing. Believe me, I know terrible flying machines. I had to deal with the most awful hot-air balloon once. But if I had had this fine machine, I'm sure I could have completed my quest without danger."

Haruto's blush reached dangerous proportions.

"There is a problem, you see," he said. "Sometimes when the glider is turning low to the ground, and I try to make it level, the turn only gets worse, and the tip of the wing hits the earth."

That sounded very familiar to Lenora, from a book called *Early Aerodynamics: Problems, Solutions, and Bitter Arguments.* "The Wright brothers had the same problem when they were working to build the first airplane," she said. "Apparently, they were finally able to solve it by inventing the first moveable rudder."

Haruto snapped his fingers. "Of course! I'm so stupid not to have thought of that!"

"You are *not* stupid," said Lenora, but Haruto had already attacked the problem, wrenching and screwing and tightening away at the tail of his glider. The ever-curious Lucy, too, was climbing all over and under the machine, fascinated by everything. Lenora sighed and went to the cockpit to have a look at the controls. The glider, she could see, was held in place by a large brick blocking the front wheel and preventing it from moving. The whole project was terribly interesting and, to get a closer look, she climbed into the cockpit.

She was just looking over the controls, trying to figure out what everything did, when suddenly she felt a horrible sensation.

The glider was moving.

At the same time, she heard Lucy ask, "What's this for?"

Lenora whipped around to see Lucy holding up the large brick in front of a horrified Haruto.

"Yikes," said Lenora.

"Lenora!" yelled Haruto, racing for the glider.

Lucy screeched and hurled herself at the glider's front wheel, trying to get the brick back in place.

But she was too late. The glider pitched right over the edge of the work area and plummeted toward the floor far below.

CHAPTER THIRTEEN
Lenora Lands

Lenora and the glider were plunging toward the floor of the Flight section. She was trying desperately to recall anything she knew about flying gliders, which was nothing. The floor was approaching at a rate she felt would certainly pulverize her and the glider both if she didn't come up with something, fast.

Then she remembered. She had never flown a glider, but she had played flight games. And to fly up, you had to pull back on the control stick, which was right in front of her. She grabbed it and pulled back as hard as she could.

The force with which the glider suddenly shot upward shoved Lenora back into her seat twice as hard as the tubes ever had. Her relief lasted only for a moment, for the glider began to fly ever more slowly. *Stalling,* thought Lenora. Thinking about the games again, she pushed the stick forward, and the glider leveled out.

Directly at a wall. Lenora yanked the stick to one side, and the glider turned, missing the wall by inches. Soon Lenora had figured out how to fly the glider in slow circles, never hitting the walls but always, always flying lower and lower. This glider had no engine and Lenora had no idea how to land, and even if she did, she didn't think she had room to do it. Sooner or later, she was going to crash.

People were starting to gather on all the different levels, watching her. One of them, Lenora saw, was the elderly woman who had been looking for Plato's *Republic,* and as the glider went by, Lenora whipped it out of her pocket and flung it at the woman, who caught it out of the air with a "Thank you!"

Now all these people started screaming instructions from different levels of the Flight section as she whizzed by, lower and lower. *Not helpful!* Lenora thought. She was trying to concentrate, and—

She saw it. A window. A large, open window, surely meant for things to fly through. She aimed right for it. Whatever was out there had to be better than what was in here, for in here she was about a minute away from a crash landing, and whatever happened, she did not want to take the chance of hurting a patron in the crash.

Out that window she went.

She gasped, all thoughts of her predicament driven momentarily out of her head.

She was hundreds, if not thousands, of feet above a massive number of huge earthen flat-topped mounds, all around for miles and miles. They all had one or more buildings on top of them, sometimes one big one, sometimes several small ones. A few of the largest mounds had even more

smaller mounds on top of them, with more buildings on top of those. It was a huge, very strange
city like nothing she'd ever seen before, not even the
metropolis of the ants, and as she looked at a long,
straight, well-kept boulevard near the largest mound
of all, she began to get an idea. Perhaps, just perhaps,
if she was very careful and very lucky, she could . . .

And then something else entirely had her complete attention. In the far, far distance, beyond
many towers, and buildings new and old, and
thousands of other structures intertwined with
tubes and bridges and causeways that made up the
Library, was the very tallest tower of them all. And
at the very top, it was burning.

*Soon enough we will eat you and that giantess and
everything else, and burn this Library to the ground
just like we did the others.*

The Library was burning. Or was it? Lenora
had a strange unease about this fire, the same
unease she felt when one of the Forces was around,
but this time it was pouring over her thousands of
times more strongly.

"Pull back on the stick to fly up!" yelled a

voice. Lenora whipped her head around. To her shock, she saw Haruto piloting a hang glider that was coming alongside her. Whereas he looked perfectly comfortable piloting that craft, Lucy, who was strapped in right beside him, did not, judging from her screaming and her white-knuckled death grip on Haruto's arm as her long scarf whipped against her face and she stared wide-eyed in utter terror at the city of mounds far below.

"And move the stick back and forth to steer," Haruto yelled over the wind.

"*I know*," shouted Lenora, slightly annoyed. How did he think she'd managed to pilot this thing out here? "I just need help landing!"

Lucy stopped screaming. "F-fly up h-higher and I'll j-jump down and help Lenora," Lucy cried out, rather bravely, Lenora thought, as she sounded like that was absolutely the last thing in the world she wanted to do.

"NO!" shouted Lenora and Haruto at the same time.

Lenora continued, to Haruto, "Land on that boulevard down there and I'll follow you in!"

Haruto looked down at the long, straight boulevard and nodded. He turned his glider and made
a wide pass over the city, descending slowly all the
while, Lenora doing her best to follow. The longer
this went on, the better she was getting, and she was
just starting to think she might want to fly around
a bit more when she realized they had passed over
the entire city. Haruto made a wide turn, Lenora following. Now they were headed straight for the boulevard. As they came back over the city, Lenora saw
a giant arch with a sign that said CAHOKIA. Haruto
flew lower and lower, until he landed right on his feet
with a few running steps. For her part, Lucy proved
that platform shoes and hang gliders do not mix, as
she immediately stumbled over them and fell. Lenora
touched down beside them and her glider rolled to
a slightly bumpy stop. Feeling disappointed that the
ride was over, she walked over to the others.

Lucy was picking herself up and dusting herself off like nothing had happened. "I'm fine! Good
landing! That was *fun!*"

"Really?" replied Lenora. "Do you always scream
in terror when you're having fun?"

"I was screaming in *fun*," cried Lucy, jumping up and down. "I want to go again! Can I get my own hang glider, *pleeease?*"

Then Lucy and Haruto both noticed the burning tower. "Is the Library on fire?" Lucy asked anxiously, forgetting all about the glider.

Lenora shook her head. "No, I don't think so. Look, there's no smoke coming from the flames, and it's not spreading. I think there's something in there. Something bad. It feels like it has to do with the Forces of Darkness."

And then Lucy was screaming again, and Lenora and Haruto whirled around to find a giant monster emerging from a hole in the ground.

CHAPTER FOURTEEN
Lenora in Cahokia

Haruto and Lucy turned and ran as Lenora stood her ground and studied the creature emerging from the hole. She had, after all, seen much worse than this, *this* being something that looked like a very giant octopus. On its (—head? She didn't know—) was a helmet that emitted a glittering field around its entire body. Each of its sixteen or so tentacles was holding advanced devices that were like nothing she had ever seen. Overall, she felt that this giant octopus-like creature had a scientific air about it and there was nothing to fear.

"Hello," she said, hoping this impressive-looking being could communicate in English. "How may I help you?"

"Hello," it replied (somehow) in a quite courteous and gentle tone. The voice seemed to come from its helmet area as the creature floated up and out of the hole and hovered about five feet above the ground. "I am relieved to see a librarian. I need help, but there are so few around, for some reason."

"I will do my best, but I should warn you, I know absolutely nothing about this place, which seems to be called Cahokia."

"Oh, have no fear about that. I am considered one of the galaxy's leading experts on all the most significant North American cities."

Now Lenora had a number of questions, as one might expect after hearing such a sentence. She decided to list them off. "The galaxy? Where are you from? What is Cahokia? And what shall I call you?"

"Ah, Lenora, my apologies for not introducing myself, as is your custom. My name is . . . well, why don't you call me Rosa. And I'm from a planet known as Zarmina's World by your scientists, in a star system they call Gliese 581. As for Cahokia, let's discuss that while we go to the scene of the crime. Will your friends be coming with us, or are they going to stay hidden behind that copper workshop on Mound 34?"

After quickly scrawling *Zarmina's World— Gliese 581—Investigate* into her notebook, Lenora called to her friends, "You can come out! It's okay. This is Rosa!"

Lucy and Haruto popped their heads around the side of a building atop a nearby mound, then walked cautiously down its steps. Reaching Lenora and Rosa, they both gulped and said, "Hello," in slightly shaky voices.

"Are you an octopus? You look like an octopus," added Lucy.

"Oh no, not at all," Rosa answered. "Although their DNA is so very strange that a few Earth scientists have suggested one explanation might be that they are descended from alien DNA, so it's within the realm of possibility that we are related to Earth octopuses."

"It's *octopi*," said Haruto.

"No, it isn't," said Lenora absently. "*Octopus* comes from Greek, not Latin, so it's not pluralized with an *i*."

"What?" asked Lucy.

"Remind me to lend you my copy of *Latin versus Greek: Battle to the Finish*," said Lenora, and, after scribbling *Possible alien DNA in octopuses? Must research* into her notebook, she said to Rosa, "You mentioned a crime?"

"Yes," said Rosa, floating down the avenue while Lenora tagged along, Lucy and Haruto staying a few cautious feet behind her. "You see, I am an archeologist who came here to study the Library's full-scale re-creation of Cahokia. Cahokia was one of the largest cities in the world during your thirteenth century, rivaling cities such as London and Paris at the time. Though it was later abandoned, no city in North America was larger until Philadelphia toward the end of your eighteenth century. Fascinating place."

Lenora was writing wildly in her notebook. "Really? Who built it?"

"Your anthropologists know them as the Mississippian culture. They thrived for eight hundred years or so, their lands and cities stretching from the Great Lakes to the Atlantic Ocean and the Gulf of Mexico, and far to the west as well. I intended to write a book about them, but a thief has stolen my notes and I have no idea how to track them down, and with my return vessel arriving soon, I don't have time to repeat my studies."

"Hmm," said Lenora. She didn't know much about solving crimes, but she was determined to give it her best shot.

They reached the foot of the very largest of the hundreds of mounds, and either ascended the steps or floated up, depending on whether they had feet or not. The mound was really quite tall and the humans were panting heavily by the time they got to the top, where they found many large buildings and terraces all around. Rosa led them into the largest of them all, which it explained had probably been the residence of Cahokia's leader.

Rosa pointed to a copper table. "I left my notes right here. Rather stupid of me, but I never imagined anyone would bother stealing them."

"Hmm," said Lenora again, thinking hard. "I suppose one of the first things you do when you are trying to solve a crime is dust for fingerprints. But I don't know how to do that and we don't have any . . . fingerprint dust or whatever, anyway."

"What is a fingerprint?" asked Rosa. Lenora showed hers to the alien.

"Ah, that's no trouble, then," said Rosa, and pointed at the top of the table with one of the many devices carried in its tentacles. Immediately, several fingerprints shone brightly. "Now what?"

"Ummm," said Lenora, who hadn't thought that far ahead. "I'm not sure. We'd need a . . . fingerprint database or something. Something to match the prints with a person."

"No trouble, either," Rosa replied, and touched another device to its helmet. The device glittered for five seconds or so. "That's odd," it said, lowering the device. "No person matching these fingerprints is anywhere in the area. But my notes were only stolen a short time ago, and I began searching for them right away."

Lenora was crestfallen. If she could not solve this mystery, then Rosa would never be able to write its book, and it sounded like a book Lenora would very much like to read. She snapped her fingers. "You said the prints didn't match a person. But what about something else? Something not a person, I mean."

"Don't only people *have* fingerprints?" asked Lucy skeptically.

"I don't know," said Lenora. "But it's worth a shot."

Rosa put the device to its helmet again, and immediately it lit up brightly. "Yes! I have a match. The fingerprints appear exactly like your human ones, but their owner is a small, furry creature with no tail, a large head with fluffy ears, and a nose shaped like a spoon."

Lenora snapped her fingers again. "I *knew* there was something suspicious about that koala."

"Yeah, me, too!" said Lucy, crossing her arms. "They've *always* looked a little suspicious to *me*. I bet they can steal anything with their little finger-print trick."

Lenora continued, "We saw it outside the Flight section a little while ago, wearing a green back-pack. Do you think you can catch it?"

"Absolutely," replied the alien. "I can locate anyone once I have their image."

Lenora scribbled *Human and koala fingerprints look exactly alike, k's could be master thieves* into her notebook and dropped it into a pocket. "Let's go get your research, then. Which way to the koala?"

"Oh," said Rosa. "I can teleport us all right to him. The trip will take no time at all." And the alien raised another of its devices.

"Wait," said Haruto. "I'd love to go . . . wherever . . . with you, Lenora, but I have to return these aircraft."

"I understand," said Lenora. "But Haruto—there is a reason you aren't seeing many librarians around. We have to catch that koala, so I don't have time to explain, but if you . . . run into any trouble, or you want to help the Library, find the

Googology section. A librarian there named Milton Sirotta can explain."

Haruto, looking a bit surprised, nodded. "I will." Then he and Lucy and Lenora hugged their goodbyes, and Haruto departed.

Lenora nodded to Rosa.

Rosa activated its device, and the three of them vanished.

The ancient city of Cahokia vanished, too, and Lenora suddenly found herself in what appeared to be a completely empty section of the Library. But there was no time to study their surroundings, for the extremely shocked-looking koala was crouched in a corner right in front of them.

The koala bolted for the exit.

"Get him!" cried Lenora, and she and Lucy threw themselves upon the thieving marsupial, each grabbing it by one of its forearms.

The koala grabbed for something wrapped around its arm as Lucy clung on.

Lenora recognized it.

"Uh-oh," she said.

Rosa made a strangled, panicked noise, and whipped something through the air into Lenora's pocket.

Everything vanished again.

A hard, thick rain pelted them. Lightning bolts cracked the sky all around. Men were running about on the deck of the wooden sailing ship upon which Lenora and Lucy were now standing, men who were shouting to one another in an unknown language as dark, massive waves crashed over the railings, soaking the girls through and through.

CHAPTER FIFTEEN
Lenora Hunts a Thief

As one might expect when one suddenly finds oneself on the pitching deck of a sailing vessel amid a terrifying storm, Lenora and Lucy immediately lost the koala they were holding as it took the opportunity to break free from their grasp and race across the soaked deck and down an open hatch.

It certainly looks like it knows where it's going, thought the part of Lenora's brain that wasn't immediately engaged in finding something to hang on to. Another pitch of the deck threw the girls into a railing, and both grabbed hold desperately.

"Where are we?" screamed Lucy over the howling wind as spray from another wave crashed over them.

"I don't know!" yelled Lenora, and was about to add *We've traveled in time!* But she quickly realized this would require too much explaining about how she was able to recognize the time machine strapped to the koala's forearm (she'd seen one before on the wrist of her time-traveling robot friend), and they really had more important concerns at the moment, such as recapturing the koala and not dying in a shipwreck.

A man in a short white robe carrying a coil of rope came stumbling by. He spotted Lenora and Lucy and stopped dead in his tracks, eyes wide. He shouted something at them, and then another pitch of the deck sent him staggering back off in the direction he'd come.

"I think we're in the ancient past or something!" screamed Lucy.

"Good guess!" yelled Lenora. Could they make their way over to the hatch and follow the koala belowdecks, she wondered, if even these men, who must be professional sailors, could barely walk? But catch the koala they must, for not only did it have Rosa's notes, but it had a time machine, and if it vanished again they'd be stranded here in the past in what looked like entirely dire circumstances.

That problem was partially resolved when the koala popped back up out of the hatch, this time carrying a wooden box that was rather too large for it to handle easily, especially when it was being chased by another sailor in a short robe, who was yelling something angrily.

"It's stealing something else!" screamed Lucy.

Obviously, thought Lenora, also thinking that whatever it was, it must be quite important, for the koala was hanging on to it tightly even though this meant it could not move very easily and could not activate its time machine. Only the wildly pitching deck was preventing it from being snatched up immediately by the man giving pursuit.

Lenora made a decision. She threw herself forward once more, this time not at the koala itself but at its green backpack, which she was sure contained Rosa's notes on the ancient North American city of Cahokia. She was also certain the koala would not be willing to give up its prizes in the backpack and box, and if she could just get control of the time machine somehow she could use it to get her and Lucy and the notes out of here and back to when they'd come from.

She grabbed hold of the backpack with a cry of victory. But the koala surprised her. It dropped the box, wriggled free from the backpack, and, as the sailor was almost upon it, evidently made the decision that its cause was lost, because it jabbed at its time machine and vanished immediately.

"Drat," said Lenora.

A blur raced by. It was Lucy, taking advantage of a momentary lull in the storm to chase after the box, which had gone spinning away across the deck. Lenora jumped up and ran after her, while the sailor who had been chasing the koala stood staring in utter astonishment at the spot where it had vanished.

Dodging a couple of sailors who were also taking advantage of the lull to try to fix something on a sail (leaving them no time to gape at what Lenora was sure was her very odd appearance), she chased after Lucy down the length of the deck.

"Come back!" she yelled, thinking that they had to at least get to a relatively safe place belowdecks while she figured out a way to escape their predicament. But Lucy was determined to get that box, and get it she did. She popped off its lid immediately.

"Oh my gosh!" she screamed, looking down at whatever was in the box. She started toward Lenora. "Lenora! This is the coolest thing I have ever—"

And that was all, for then Lucy stepped into a puddle of water in her platform shoes, her feet went out from under her, and she and the box went over the railing and into the wine-dark sea.

Freezing cold water crashed over Lenora as she dove into the waters. She had given it no thought whatsoever before diving over the railing after Lucy, but on the way down she realized she had no idea if the other girl could even swim. Though Lenora was not about to abandon her friend anyway, leaving aside the fact that their situation, bad already, had just gotten immeasurably worse.

Fortunately, Lucy *could* swim. For when Lenora

surfaced, struggling a bit in her dress and still gripping the koala's backpack (fortunate also that not only could Lenora swim, but was in fact quite a good swimmer), she could see Lucy bobbing in the water, paddling desperately, only a very short distance away. Knowing that they could easily be separated in the rough seas, she kicked toward Lucy and put the arm holding the backpack around the girl as she paddled with her free hand.

Lucy seemed on the verge of tears. "Lenora," she screamed. "I'm so sorry. I lost the box! It sank."

"Forget about the box!" yelled Lenora. She was busy looking desperately for the ship. Despair crashed through her as she saw that it had already drifted quite far from them, and in a few more moments had disappeared almost entirely from sight. There was absolutely no way she and Lucy could swim back to it.

An enormous wave came up, and for a moment both girls went underwater. When they resurfaced, sputtering, Lenora almost losing her grip on her friend, she wondered if she should drop the backpack, and then wondered if it even mattered, for there was no help in sight and the two of them were not likely to make it for long in these rough, cold seas.

"What should we do?" screamed Lucy.

It did not help a bit, thought Lenora, that Lucy seemed to harbor no doubts at all that Lenora had a fix for this situation. She hated to disappoint her—and then she felt something bump into her leg. And she remembered:

Rosa, making a strangled, panicked noise, and whipping something through the air into Lenora's pocket.

Rosa had known exactly what was about to happen, just as Lenora had.

Kicking hard to stay afloat, Lenora stabbed her hand into her pocket. When it came back up, she was holding another of the alien archeologist's glittering devices, this one the size and shape of a large and heavy pen displaying a lot of swiftly changing symbols that Lenora did not recognize, and one thing she did recognize—a button.

"That's Rosa's thing!" screamed Lucy. "I think you should

CHAPTER SIXTEEN
Lenora and Ada

press it!"

But Lenora, of course, had already pressed the button on Rosa's device, and by the time Lucy finished her unnecessary suggestion both girls were sitting on the Library floor in front of the floating alien, who was waving each of its sixteen or so tentacles in what seemed like a happy fashion.

"It is with relief," said Rosa, "that I see you ascertained the purpose of my device."

"Not exactly," said Lenora, panting from exertion. A large pool of water was collecting around the girls, dripping from their clothes. "But you had obviously given it to me for a reason."

"Yes. That"—and here Rosa used an alien word that Lenora did not understand—"will return objects and persons to me from anywhere they might be. I was sure you would return, but I am surprised to see you also recovered my notes in the process. Extraordinary."

"I was not going to lose your notes," said Lenora, handing the device and backpack over to the alien, who accepted both with one of its tentacles. "I hope they are waterproof and fireproof, like my notebook."

"Naturally," replied Rosa.

"The koala tried to steal something else, too," said Lucy sadly. "But I lost it. It sank to the bottom of the sea." She shivered, crossing both arms around herself.

"You must be cold," said the alien. "Here." It pointed another device, there was a flash, and the girls found themselves completely dry.

"Geez," said Lucy. "Is there anything you *can't* do?"

"Quite a bit," said Rosa, but Lenora was not listening to this conversation. For she was looking past the archeologist now, and seeing that what had once been an empty section of the Library was now anything but. The room was rather small for a Library section, but the formerly bare walls were now covered with images of watery and badly corroded dials, gears, pins, and cranks, some of them looking like a partially assembled mechanism of some kind, and some simply lying on cloths on their own. Some of them had inscriptions on them that looked rather Greek-ish to Lenora.

In the middle of the room was a large table, and on that table was a giant cloth, and on that cloth were many bronze fragments that looked very much like cleaned-up versions of the things in the images.

Lucy had noticed them, too. "Hey," she said, "that stuff looks really familiar."

There was something else on the tablecloth. Pieces of a box, partially reassembled, with many parts missing, but looking much like a broken-up version of a box Lenora had seen only moments (or perhaps thousands of years, depending on how you looked at it) before.

"Uh-oh," said Lenora to Rosa. "I think we might have changed history." She was worried now, for in books, changing history was almost never good.

"Do not fear," replied Rosa. "We all change history with everything we do. This is why we should consider our actions carefully, as each one will affect the future to come. Should we join Lucy?"

For Lucy had gone straight to the table, next to a puzzled-looking librarian who was peering down at the assorted fragments, his chin in his hand, deep in thought. So deep that he had completely failed to notice two girls and an alien who had popped out of nowhere—or had they? Lenora was not sure how history changes worked exactly. But she was sure now that the objects on the table had been in the same box that Lucy had lost in the sea.

Giving up (for the moment) on figuring out how

history changing worked, Lenora went over to the table, Rosa beside her. She cleared her throat. "Excuse me," she said to Cosmo (for that was the name on the librarian's badge).

Cosmo flinched and, looking up, suddenly noticed Lenora and the others. "Oh!" he said. "My apologies. I have been studying the Antikythera mechanism so intently that I frequently fail to notice things around me."

"That's all right," said Lenora. "So what exactly is this . . . Anti-kith-uh . . ."

"An-tee-KITH-ur-uh," said Cosmo. "It is a small Greek island, near which this ancient mechanism was discovered, all broken up into pieces at the bottom of the Aegean Sea. It is estimated to have been lost to the waters around 100 BC."

"Sorry about that," said Lucy.

"So what does it do?" asked Lenora hurriedly.

Giving Lucy a strange look, Cosmo continued, "Well, if it were ever to be assembled, one could use it to predict the movements of many astronomical objects and events, such as the sun, and phases of the moon, and perhaps even the locations of planets."

"Perhaps?" said Lenora.

"Yes," sighed Cosmo. "You see, we've never been quite sure, because we'd never found all the pieces. As the world's first known mechanical computer, however, the mechanism is of great interest. Knowledge of how to create such an intricate machine was lost in antiquity and not rediscovered until the fourteenth century. And so I was sent on a Library expedition to find the missing bits, like the crank that operates the entire thing. The expedition was successful, but now that I've got all the pieces collected and cleaned and patched up, I have no idea how they all fit together. It's a mystery that I fear we may never—"

"Like this," said Lucy.

Everyone turned toward the girl. Everyone, even Rosa, gasped in astonishment.

For sitting in front of Lucy was the reassembled mechanism, gears whirling and dials spinning as Lucy turned its crank.

"Lucy!" Lenora cheered.

"What?" yelped Cosmo. "But . . . you . . . how?!"

Lucy shrugged. "It's no big deal. It's not like I haven't seen it befo—"

"Still," interrupted Lenora. "I can't believe you just put it all together like that!"

"Amazing indeed," said Rosa.

Lucy shrugged again. "Nah. I like taking stuff apart and putting it back together. That's how I fixed my toaster. And once I took Daddy's watch apart and put it back together. It didn't work after that, though. I guess it was pretty expensive, because he—"

"Marvelous!" cried Cosmo. "Simply incredible. You are a regular Ada L—"

Lucy stopped cranking. And she gave Cosmo a look as cold as the waters of the ancient Aegean Sea, freezing him mid-word. "What. Did. You. Say?"

Cosmo faltered. "I . . . I was only going to say you remind me of Ada—"

"HOW DO YOU KNOW MY NAME?" shouted Lucy.

Everything went silent as Lucy's shout echoed around the room.

Finally, Lenora spoke. "That's your real name?"

she asked gently. "Why do you hate it? I think it's beautiful."

Lucy softened. "I'm sorry," she said to Cosmo. "I just really hate that name. It's boring and dull and I don't want to be boring and dull. I want to be special and amazing, like Lenora."

"Oh dear," said Lenora.

"But it's not boring and dull at all," said Rosa. "I believe Cosmo meant to compare you to Ada Lovelace."

Cosmo nodded.

"Who's that?" asked Lucy skeptically.

"She was a young human who is quite the legend on my planet and yours," replied Rosa. "She wrote humanity's first published computer program in Earth year 1843, before a computer that could run it had even been created. And she was the first human to recognize all the things computers might someday do besides just calculating numbers. As you just reassembled your world's oldest computer at not much more than a glance, I can see why Cosmo might think of her."

Lucy looked around at all of them. "Really?"

she said softly, her voice breaking. "*I* make you think of someone like *that*?"

"Quite," said Rosa.

"Certainly," said Cosmo.

"Why not?" asked Lenora with a smile.

Lucy sniffled and wiped her arm across her nose. "Thanks. It's just—I mean, Daddy tells me how great I am all the time, but I don't think he really pays much attention to anything I actually do. And I've never had any real friends. Just the people Daddy calls our servants."

"Well," said Lenora, "you have lots of friends now. And now that you know how cool your name is . . . do you still want us to call you Lucy?"

Now it was Lucy/Ada's turn to put her chin on her hand and think. She thought and thought, and then she spoke. "I want to be Ada," she said, her voice full of wonder. "I'm Ada!"

Cosmo and Rosa cheered as Lenora patted her friend on the arm. "Ada it is," she said. "Now, we must continue on. Rosa, I don't suppose our history change . . . changed anything else, did it?"

Rosa was silent for a moment, lights flashing

on and off all over its helmet. "No," it said at last. "The Library at large is just as it was."

Lenora sighed and beckoned Cosmo down so she could whisper. "Do you have any idea where we can find Zenodotus?"

Cosmo, seeming to understand, whispered back. "No. I have only heard stories about him. He is described as a powerhouse of courage, with green eyes and a pair of old spectacles, always fighting for the Library against its enemies. Which is quite extraordinary, considering how the Library of Alexandria was ruined when Marc Antony gave away all its manuscripts to Cleopatra. Or so I've heard."

Lenora sighed again. She did not even bother writing this latest tale down in her notebook. "Now that the Antikythera mechanism has been assembled," she whispered, "I suggest you find Milton Sirotta in Googology. He'll tell you more when you get there."

Cosmo straightened and nodded. "Thank you, Lenora," he said, and rushed out of the room.

And then it hit her. Something Rosa had said earlier . . . Hoping against hope, Lenora asked with a tremor, "Rosa—you said you can locate anyone once you have their image. Can you find a man named Zenodotus?" Quickly, she described what she knew about him to Rosa, about his distinctive mustache and blue robe, and his energy and vigor and strength and green eyes and old spectacles.

Rosa touched device to helmet, which lit up instantly. "Yes. I have located him."

Lenora almost fell to the floor. "Where is he? Can you send us to him?"

"Yes. Though . . ." Rosa hesitated. "He has changed somehow. He is not quite as he was described. I'm unable to tell you more."

Lenora nodded. "We'll figure it out when we get there. Let's go!"

"I will teleport you there," replied Rosa. "But I am afraid I cannot come with you. For now that I have my notes, I must meet my ship. It is time for me to go home."

Lenora nodded again. "I understand," she said. "But just in case anything goes wrong . . ." And she whispered to Rosa about Milton Sirotta and Googology.

"Thank you," said Rosa. "I will remember."

"Thank *you!*" said Lenora. "Good luck with your book, and do send me a copy!"

"I will," said Rosa. And the alien pointed yet another device at Lenora and Lucy, or rather Ada.

The girls vanished.

CHAPTER SEVENTEEN
Lenora's Light

Something was wrong. Rosa had said it would teleport Lenora and Ada to meet Zenodotus at last. But instead of standing before the dashing and courageous librarian, they were standing in one of the offices Lenora had seen when she'd first arrived. And it was completely empty, with no desk, shelves, or windows. Lenora immediately tried the door.

It was locked.

From behind them came a popping sound, and a cough. The girls whipped around.

A startling sight met them. It was a young girl, younger than Ada even, and she was dressed in a long purple raincoat. In her hand she held a device with a single button, which she was pressing firmly. Lenora's arms prickled with goose bumps, as had happened with the woman in the red raincoat and the man in the green. She knew it could be no coincidence, but she hadn't time to think on it further, as the girl crept closer and spoke.

"Little Lenora," the girl chuckled, in a voice that suggested a much older being. "I sensed some sort of teleportation involving you, and I have interrupted it in order to bring you wonderful news."

Lenora's heart began to pound. Whatever this news was, she was certain it was anything but wonderful.

"Now wait just a minute," announced Ada. "What are you, seven years old? We need to find your parents!"

The girl ignored her, staring directly at Lenora. "The resistance of the Assistant Answerer—that Malachi woman—has been discovered. And so—

we ate her. The soul of such a being was most delicious."

"No," whispered Lenora in horror. This couldn't be. Malachi devoured? Then everything was lost.

"Malachi?" said Ada skeptically. "That ten-foot-tall woman? No way you could devour her, whatever that means."

"No, it's true," Lenora continued in a whisper. "I can feel it. She's gone."

The girl in the raincoat continued, "And the Director has finally fired the last of the librarians, including you."

"What?!" shouted Ada. "Daddy wouldn't fire Lenora!"

The girl ignored her.

Lenora knew it was true. She could feel it. She was no longer a librarian. She had no right to be here any longer.

The girl reached out her hand. "Now, come with me. You must be . . . escorted . . . from the premises."

"Don't do it!" seethed Ada. "I'll talk to Daddy. None of this is true!"

Lenora reached out to take the girl's hand. It was time, she knew, to leave.

"No!" shouted Ada, and swatted the girl's hand away. The girl dropped the device, which went clattering across the floor, and she leapt after it with a scream, and—

The girl and the office and everything else vanished.

Now Ada and Lenora were no longer standing in an ugly, neon-lit office. Instead, they found themselves in a vast and dimly lit room. The only light came from torches flickering weakly along the walls. The tall double doors behind them were padlocked, and the view down the length of the room was obscured by the darkness and by the many tall columns holding up the ceiling high above. Along the walls were alcoves stuffed with scrolls, and around the floor were scattered many old, dusty objects, like shields and small carved animals and old paintings. The whole place felt like an abandoned museum, but of course Lenora knew it was not abandoned. Someone must be keeping the torches lit.

"What happened back there?" whispered Ada. This felt like a place where one must whisper.

"I don't know," said Lenora quietly. "But thank you. I can see now that those were lies. I don't know why I couldn't tell at the time."

Ada nodded. "I'm just glad we're out of there. That kid gave me the creeps. So where do we go now?"

"Forward," Lenora whispered. "There's nowhere else to go."

The two girls walked, their footsteps echoing around and around. Soon they could make out a little bubble of light at the far end of the room, and as they drew closer they saw a man sitting at a desk piled with papers that seemed dangerously close to several lit candles. He was wearing a blue robe and was slumped forward with his face in his hands. Beside him was an inkpot with a feathery quill dipped inside.

"Zenodotus?" said Lenora cautiously.

The man threw himself back in his chair, wide-eyed with alarm, and the girls recoiled.

"What?" he cried. "How? How did you get in

here?" Then he collapsed back in his chair, one hand over his heart.

Lenora looked him over. He had a shock of brown hair that curled into a sharp tip, ancient spectacles on the end of his nose, and, of course, an elaborate mustache that curled at both ends.

"We were transferred here," Lenora explained, "by an alien archeologist from Zarmina's World in the Gliese 581 star system."

"Of course," mused the man, who seemed to be recovering. "I should have thought of that. But how do you know who I am? And why did you come here?"

Lenora hesitated, looking all around.

"Do not worry," said Zenodotus. "There are no listening devices here. The Forces of Darkness do not know of this place, and even if they did, they stopped bothering with me some time ago."

"Malachi told me to find you," said Lenora. "I don't know why. But it must have something to do with the Library being taken over by the Forces."

"Malachi," sighed Zenodotus. "I told her I did not wish to be found ever again."

"But why? Don't you want to help take the Library back?"

"Lenora, the Library is being lost because of me. For thousands of years, the Library has been overseen by the Board, a body of three of the wisest and most honorable of all librarians. The membership changed from time to time, and it was my job to ensure the Board's sanctity as it changed. But I failed."

"Something happened?" ventured Lenora.

"Yes. I was not able to see through the deceptions of the newest members. They appeared to me as clever, and cautious, and strong, and I was easily fooled. And so it is I who have brought us nearly to destruction."

"But how?" asked Lenora. "What changed for you?"

Ada leaned toward Lenora, whispering with the side of her hand covering her mouth. "He said he's, like, thousands of years old. Maybe he's, y'know, losing it."

"Shush!" said Lenora.

Ada shushed.

"I have suffered many defeats, children," Zenodotus replied, his voice shaking. "Too many to count. I lost at the great Library of Alexandria, and I lost at the House of Wisdom in Baghdad. And so many more—the Library of Banu Ammar, and Madrassah, and the Maya codices, and the libraries of the Kings of Burma . . ." He faltered, placing his hand over his face. "For a long time I was able to maintain the same spirit Malachi still possesses, a spirit that I see you possess as well. But then the defeats overwhelmed me, and I lost that most precious and wonderful thing. I lost it so gradually I did not realize it was leaving me. And during this time, this distracted and heart-wrenching time, the Board was infiltrated by the Forces, and I did not see it. And thus my defeat was final."

Lenora and Ada were silent for a long moment.

"Maybe if you cleaned up around here," started Ada, until Lenora silenced her with a venomous look.

Then Lenora spoke. *"Knowledge Is a Light.* Don't you remember this?"

Zenodotus nodded. "I do. But the light is no longer within me."

"How can that be?" Lenora cried. The light was in her, she knew, and she could not imagine the horror of losing it. Surely such a thing was impossible. "You must have it, somewhere. Something must be left!"

Zenodotus shook his head. "I wish it were. But I am lost, young ones. Lost to time, lost to the fight."

Lenora closed her eyes. She thought back to the battle she and Malachi had fought against the hideous monstrosity in the History of Science section. The battle during which she had glowed. She thought of her terror in the face of the woman in the red raincoat, and how she herself had glowed (she was sure of it now) when she had remembered Malachi's words. When she opened her eyes again, she was indeed glowing once more, and more strongly than before.

Ada spoke up. "Lenora, I hate to tell you, but you're uh . . . glowing. Is that bad, or . . . ?"

Lenora smiled at Ada. "No, it is not bad at all. Quite the opposite." She reached out her hands to

Zenodotus. "Take some of mine, Zenodotus. I will give you strength."

Zenodotus's eyes began to water. "I don't know if I can."

Lenora leaned over his desk, reaching for his hands. "Try."

Zenodotus closed his eyes and took Lenora's hands.

"Knowledge Is a Light, Zenodotus," whispered Lenora, her glow brightening. "Throughout history, that light has at times burned very dimly, and nearly even gone out, as it has for you, while in other times it has blazed up gloriously, as it will for you once more."

Her words echoed, again and again, growing stronger with each bounce off every wall and ceiling, until it was Lenora's voice, repeating again and again, with the commanding force of a thousand Lenoras, the words: *KNOWLEDGE IS A LIGHT!*

Zenodotus leapt from his seat, releasing Lenora's hands, gazing at her in amazement as tears streamed down his cheeks. And she could see, coming from him, the faintest glow.

The man looked at his hands. "How?" he asked. "I didn't think . . . I never knew . . ."

Ada, backed up against a nearby column, yelped. "Wow. Lenora, you've got, like, magic powers and stuff! Why didn't you tell me?"

Lenora stumbled back, suddenly weary, and plopped down onto the floor. She was no longer glowing, but she could still feel that strength inside her. She locked eyes with Zenodotus. "Can you help us now?"

"Yes," replied Zenodotus. "Yes. I think I can."

CHAPTER EIGHTEEN
Lenora Loses

"Good!" said Lenora to Zenodotus, who was still staring at the faint glow coming from his hands. "You can come with us, and we'll get Malachi, too, and then we'll take down the Director and the Board—" She stopped at the distraught look on Ada's face.

"You wouldn't hurt Daddy, would you?" Ada said, tearing up. "I know he's—made some mistakes, but . . . he means well. I think."

Lenora softened. "Of course not," she said. "We aren't going to hurt anyone. But we must take back the Library, Ada. You know this. And we cannot do this with your father giving the orders."

The girl nodded, wiping her arm across her eyes.

"Well?" said Lenora to Zenodotus, whose tears had dried up. "Let's go!"

To her surprise, the ancient librarian sat down heavily in his chair, the faintest smile on his face. "Oh, Lenora. I'm afraid I cannot. For many reasons."

"But why? Your light has returned! And you said you would help us."

Zenodotus nodded. "And I will. But Lenora, you must understand—you are much stronger than me. And though you have given me much, it is your time to defeat the Forces. Even if I had your full strength, which would be extraordinary, I would be doing the Library a disservice by stepping in your way. You represent the future, Lenora. You must now learn to lead the battle on your own. If you do not, there is no future for the Library."

"Then *how* are you going to help us?" cried Lenora in desperation. "I can't defeat the Forces on my own!" She did not see how she could possibly do this, when even Malachi could not.

Zenodotus leaned back in his chair, put his fingers to his temples, and closed his eyes. "What do you mean, alone? What about the army you have assembled?"

"Army?" said Lenora, puzzled. "I don't have any army."

Zenodotus looked at her in surprise. "What do you mean? They are gathered in Googology, waiting for you."

"Lenora's rebel base!" said Ada.

"Yes, Lenora," said Zenodotus. "You seem unaware of the success of your efforts to guide librarians to safety. Word of your—rebel base, as Ada says—spread rapidly from one librarian to the next. The ones who remain are all there now."

"So they can defeat the Forces?" Lenora asked.

Zenodotus shook his head. "No," he said. "They are still greatly outnumbered. And the Director still holds thrall over the Library's patrons."

Ada made a strangled cry at these words.

"I am sorry," said Zenodotus to Ada. "But even as the Library is coming apart, many patrons believe it is not only improving, but becoming stronger.

Your father is telling them this. As long as they still listen, he is in control."

"I'll talk to him," said Ada desperately. "He'll listen once I've explained everything."

Lenora gave a weary sigh. "Is there anything else you can do to help?" she asked Zenodotus.

Zenodotus nodded. "Yes." He reached behind his neck and loosened a small chain, and then drew from within his robe an object that was clearly a Tube key—but this one had an air of great age, and strange runes were carved all over it. "This is my Tube key. I have not used it in many years. You can have it. It is a key like no other. You will find that it will take you anywhere in the Library you want to go. You are no longer limited by section. Which is well, as the lights are going out all over the Library, section by section. There is a tube right outside those doors. It has not been used in a long time, but I expect it will still operate. They were built well."

Lenora accepted the key with great reverence, feeling it tingle in her palm. "Thank you," she said. "But what are you going to do? You really ought to contribute to the fight somehow. You can't just sit here. Also, you need to move those papers away from those candles unless you want to burn the place down."

Zenodotus chuckled and slid the stacks around to wiser positions. "Yes. I have decided exactly what I will do. The best way for me to contribute to the fight against lies, fear, and hate is to tell your story."

"My story?" asked Lenora. She had not realized she had a story. But looking back, she supposed she did.

"Yes. It has been centuries since I put quill to parchment. But you have inspired many here, Lenora. It is my hope you will now inspire others." He took a deep breath. "Next, I must decide on a pseudonym. None in the world beyond will believe that Zenodotus, first librarian of Alexandria, still lives."

"I'm sure you'll think of something," said Lenora encouragingly. "But now—I think we really must get moving. Can you let us out?"

"Of course." Zenodotus stood and proceeded to the padlocked doors, the girls following.

"Do you think he'll put me in the story?" whispered Ada to Lenora.

Lenora smiled. "Of course. You're an important part of it, after all."

The girl beamed in pleasure, though Lenora could still see deep sadness in her eyes.

They came to the doors. Zenodotus produced a very large and old key from within his robes and opened the padlocks. The big wooden doors swung open, protesting all this with an enormous creaking.

The corridor beyond was dark, and smelled damp and musty in a way that told one the place had not been entered in a long time. But at a great distance down the corridor, Lenora could see the glint of light on copper. A tube.

Zenodotus turned to the girls with a smile. "Thank you, Lenora. And thank you, too, Ada. You are right. I need to get this place cleaned up. Now, off you go. The Library needs you."

Lenora and Ada nodded. There seemed little more to say, and so Lenora made her way cautiously down the long corridor, wary of running into anything. Ada crept along beside her. Behind them, the doors closed with a creaking crash, and Lenora could hear the sound of padlocks locking.

Then Lenora groaned. She had completely forgotten to ask Zenodotus what had really happened to the Library of Alexandria. Oh, well. Another time . . .

Onward they went.

They walked for a long time. Somehow it seemed they were never getting any closer to that glint on copper. But at last, Lenora could see they were drawing near. And then—

Goose bumps on her arms.

Blinding lights all around.

A terrible crashing.

A hard shove from behind, propelling Lenora forward with a stumble.

And she thought, her eyes closed tight against the glare:

Something fell.

Ada was screaming. "Lenora! Help!"

Lenora whipped around, blinking, trying to see.

Metal bars had crashed down, separating her and Ada. And beside the girl were two of the Forces, the man in the green raincoat and the woman in the red, grinning sharp-toothed grins and gripping Ada by the arms as she struggled and kicked. Lenora realized that they'd have had her, too, if not for Ada's shove. And as she realized that, she also realized that panic was surging through her and her feet felt rooted to the floor, just as had happened when she first met the woman in the red raincoat.

"Lucky you had your friend here to save you," the woman said to Lenora, "but you will have her assistance no longer."

"We'll be back for you," said the man.

With three popping sounds, they vanished.

Her fear evaporating just as quickly as it had come, Lenora threw herself against the bars, reaching for where her friend had been only moments before. "Ada!" she screamed. "No!"

But she was gone.

Lenora was alone.

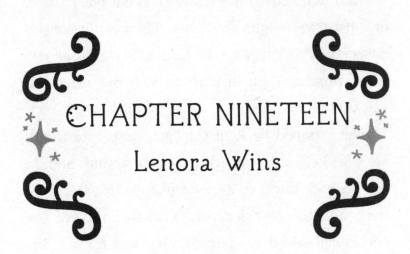

CHAPTER NINETEEN
Lenora Wins

She raced to the tube and threw open the door.

She had to rescue Ada. Zenodotus had said his key would take her wherever she wanted, and she wanted Ada. And so there was, of course, a label blinking ADA with a slot below it.

Lenora fumbled for the key, then thrust it forward.

And stopped, inches away from plunging the key into the slot.

Something felt wrong. Lenora thought hard. She did not know where the Forces had taken Ada.

She did not know how many of them were there, or what traps might await her. Though she longed desperately to hurry to the rescue, it would be terribly stupid to rush in without knowing what she was up against.

She slumped back in the seat, desperate. Ada's cries for help still echoed in Lenora's mind. Should she go back and ask Zenodotus? No, there wasn't time, and the corridor was blocked anyway. The Forces had said they were coming back for her. She had to get out of there.

And then she had it. She knew where she wanted to go. And so, naturally, the ADA label changed:

THE DIRECTOR.

Lenora thrust the key home, and shot off into the darkness.

When she got to the Director's office, she was ready. The moment the door opened, she bolted from the tube and straight up the golden staircase, right past a startled member of the Forces, who made a grab for her but lost his balance and tumbled down the steps as Lenora thought, *They've got to start protecting this place better,* and then she was in the office of the Director, surrounded by Forces, all closing in on her.

And just as they were about to snatch her, she yelled, "Princess has been kidnapped!"

The Director, who had been smiling giddily and polishing his platinum DIRECTOR badge while he watched one of his own speeches on the transmission console, instantly went grim. "What?" he said, looking straight at Lenora. "What are you talking about?"

"Nothing, sir!" said a member of the Forces, this one having the appearance of a teenage girl who had hold of Lenora's right arm. "This girl is crazy."

"She's lying," said a man who had Lenora's left wrist. "You know how females are."

"Then where is she?" shouted Lenora. "Where's Princess?"

The Director stood, his voice booming. "Let go of her! Now!"

With great reluctance, one by one, the Forces released Lenora, glaring as she glared back.

"Now," said the Director with great authority. "Where is my daughter?"

"I saw her just now, playing with the dinosaurs," said a woman. "She's fine. Very happy."

The Director paused. Lenora could see he was becoming confused. "Why don't you ask them to get her, then?" Lenora asked. "She can go back to the dinosaurs when she's done."

"She's very happy," said the woman soothingly. "Why would we interrupt your precious Princess over this disrespectful, loud little girl?"

Lenora saw the Director hesitating, unsure. "Princess hasn't seen you in a while," she said carefully. "That poor girl . . . imagine how hard it must be to be away from a father as wonderful as you."

The man behind Lenora hissed. She did not flinch.

"Of course!" said the Director, straightening. "She must miss me terribly! Go fetch my Princess at once!"

None of the Forces moved. Instead, they all looked at one another. And Lenora saw things begin to slither under their clothes.

"Did you hear me?" shouted the Director, coming around his desk to the front of the dais. "I order you to bring me Princess!"

The Forces faced the Director. "We can't do that," one of them said. The usual tone of fake respect was fading. "The presence of your daughter . . . distracts you. Interferes with your judgment. Causes you to forget the Plan."

The Director's fists began to shake. His face turned red, then purple. The veins in his neck and forehead bulged. Lenora had seen this before, and knew he was about to fly into a rage at such disobedience.

And she knew exactly what to do.

The attention of the Forces was entirely on the Director. And so she slipped away, then sidled along the wall until she came to the Transmission Console. And flipped a switch from OFF to LIVE.

Unbeknownst to anyone but Lenora, the scene was now broadcasting to the entire Library.

"I am the Director!" the Director shrieked at the Forces. "Do you know how many companies I've run? Do you know how much money I make? *You* work for *me*, and *you* do what I say!"

The man facing him continued calmly, "This *girl* is destroying the Plan—"

"Don't you tell me about the Plan!" screeched the Director. From the color on his face to his bulging veins, Lenora was worried that he might explode. "The Plan was *my* idea!"

"Was it?" mused the man. "I seem to recall visiting you and telling you that we could make you the biggest, most important, most famous librarian of all time. You were quite pleased at the notion."

Lenora did not think it possible to screech at a pitch any higher than the one he already had, but the Director found a way. "I don't need you idiots! I'm the smartest genius in the world. I could do this all by myself. You're fired! You're *all* fired! Now where is my daughter?"

"We took her to the Board. They can protect her."

"I can protect her better than anyone! Bring her to me!"

"No," said the man, quite simply.

And that was when something inside the Director broke loose. With incoherent screeching, he turned to the nearest portrait of himself, tore it from the wall, and hurled it at the man, who easily ducked under it.

The Director stalked around the room, ripping each portrait from the wall and throwing them at the Forces. His rage grew ever wilder as they easily dodged these attacks.

"I am the Director!" he continued to screech. "I'm the smartest! You're all idiots! Everyone is an idiot! Everyone except *me*!"

At last, the final portrait was hurled. The Director, panting and purple, looked around for something else to destroy, then slumped against the wall, exhausted.

"I'm the Director," he croaked.

"You see," said the man, "this is why you have us. We need you to appear to everyone as the tough, confident leader of the Library. And you need us to protect you from being seen like . . . this. You are fortunate such outbursts are kept hidden."

"No," said Lenora. All heads turned to her, only now noticing her next to the transmission console. She gestured to the panel. "Everyone has seen it. Everyone in the Library. All the Library's patrons.

You put those monitors everywhere, because you wanted everyone to see all of your lies. But now they have seen the truth."

The face of every one of the Forces went ashen. "No," a man said. "The Board . . . they'll—"

As one, all of them opened their mouths to scream. And then each of them was—Lenora was not able to describe it quite like anything else—*pulled* from the room, as though pulled through keyholes. *Like the opposite of a balloon popping,* she'd later say. Only the beginning of their screams was left.

"Help me," choked a voice from behind her.

She turned to see the Director on his knees, his face white, his hands clasped, imploring. "Help me," he said again to Lenora. "You have to help me get Princess back. I'm the Director . . . I'm the Director . . ."

"Not anymore," Lenora said, pointing to his chest. His glittering platinum DIRECTOR badge was gone. "You're fired."

CHAPTER TWENTY
Lenora Flies Again

The Not-Director gaped helplessly. "I can't . . . they can't . . . you can't . . . I order you to . . . to . . ."

Lenora drew back in disgust. It was hard for her to believe that she had ever thought this man would have the authority to force Ada's return. But now she knew where Ada was, and what she would have to do.

"Did you hear me?" rasped the Not-Director. "I *order* you to—"

"You're not ordering me to do anything," said

Lenora. "I'm going to face the Board and save Ada—you're not calling her Princess anymore—because she's my friend. And I'm going to restore the Library. And I'm not going to do it alone."

She cleared her throat, then spoke to the transmission console. "Message to Googology. This is Lenora. Everyone—the Director has been fired. It's time for us to bring the fight to the Forces of Darkness. While I'm dealing with the Board, I need the rest of you to start putting books back on the shelves." And then, hoping against hope that she was right, she continued, "We're going to win today, and the Forces will not soon forget it." She had no idea what she would find when she met the Board, but she had learned early on that it was important to project confidence in the face of fear. And though she was indeed afraid, she knew she had no choice but to find a way to win. She reached behind the machine and pulled the plug because, after all, it would no longer be needed when the monitors were gone and the books and everything else in the Library were returned to their proper places.

She turned to leave, and to her surprise, the

Not-Director was gathering himself. He was back on his feet with a savage expression on his face, straightening his tie. He seemed to have forgotten Lenora was there. "Can't fire me," he was muttering to himself. "I'm the Director. I'm the best, smartest librarian. I'll tell the Board a thing or two about those disloyal employees they gave me. Tell 'em they'd better remember who's in charge, or they're all fired! All of them!"

Lenora sighed and strode through the doors and down the steps. To her annoyance, she found the Not-Director was following her. "What are you doing?" she demanded.

The Not-Director, who obviously still considered himself to be in charge, stuck his finger in Lenora's face. "You're taking me to the Board."

Lenora did not have time to argue. She turned to the open tube. "Fine. Squeeze yourself in behind the chair and get ready for a rough ride."

"*I* am taking the chair," said the Director. "You sit in back. You work for me."

Lenora looked at him. "Do you know how to operate the tubes?"

He looked at Lenora.

She looked at him.

They looked at each other.

The Not-Director crossed his arms and looked off to the side with a petulant pout. "No."

"Then get in back," said Lenora, climbing into the chair. "And be quick about it."

The Not-Director squeezed in back, muttering all the time about how this was going to ruin his suit and Lenora was going to face disciplinary action, and a bunch of other nonsense that Lenora was no longer paying attention to. For the very first and very last time, Lenora felt some sympathy for those poor Forces, who had had to spend all their days listening to this (here Lenora used a very unkind term, which will not be repeated despite its complete accuracy) go on and on. And on.

There was now, of course, a large label reading THE BOARD in bright letters. As the Not-Director continued his babbling, the capsule, to Lenora's great surprise, did not shoot off down its glass tunnel when she inserted the key Zenodotus had given her. Instead, it rose gently into the air. Lenora looked up. Above them, a door was opening in the ceiling. The capsule rose up and through, and soon they were in open sky. Ahead of them was a tower. Lenora looked up and up and up. The top of the tower was surrounded by flames.

She flinched at a hideous screeching next to her right ear. Somehow the Not-Director had managed to twist himself around so he could see out the windows. "What are you doing? Make it go down!"

"Shhh," said Lenora. "I'm flying this tube and it requires my complete concentration. If you are not perfectly silent, I'll probably lose control and we'll crash and die horridly."

The Not-Director clammed up immediately. The silence was delightful beyond words.

Lenora looked back up at the tower. The tube continued to float toward its flaming top, leaving her with little doubt that this tower housed the Board. She also had little doubt that she had no idea what she was getting into, that she knew nothing about the Board, and that her bravado back in the Not-Director's office was perhaps misplaced. She tried to console herself with the fact that an army of librarians was now in open revolt, and that someone would think of something, even if she couldn't.

The flames drew near. Lenora became concerned. Though they didn't seem to be actually burning anything, she wondered what effect they might have on the capsule and its passengers. To her relief, an opening appeared just beneath the flames, a bit of the stone tower wall sliding aside. The capsule floated through, came to a stop on the stone floor, and opened. Lenora got out to find that they were in a large, round room, all stone, completely empty but for a rather dizzyingly tall ladder that went up to the ceiling, ending at a trapdoor.

There was a tumbling sound as the Not-Director fell out of the tube behind her. He picked himself up and began patting his suit, muttering his list of complaints and threats once more. Lenora was reaching her limits with this man.

She marched toward the ladder, for there was nowhere else to go.

"We have to climb *that*?" shrieked the Not-Director. "I'm not climbing. I want an elevator."

"Maybe you can find one out there," said Lenora, jerking a thumb at the open door leading out into empty sky. "Meanwhile, I'm going up." Then she had a thought. "Though the Board probably expects the most important person to be in front."

This worked perfectly. The Not-Director pushed past her, as though terrified that Lenora might take the lead, and began to climb. Lenora allowed him a generous head start. Whatever was up there, she'd rather have the Not-Director climb into it first.

The Not-Director was at it again. "Stupid Board! So disrespectful. I should have come here before so they could see who they were dealing with!"

"Wait," said Lenora from below. "You've never met the Board?"

"No," snarled the Not-Director. "I've never met the king of Canada either! Who cares! I can't possibly let *everyone* who works for me have that privilege."

Now Lenora was even more glad the Not-Director was going first.

He reached the top, Lenora ten feet or so below

him, not looking down, though she'd grown quite used to heights by now. The Not-Director shoved the trapdoor wide open, clambered through, straightened himself—

—and began to scream.

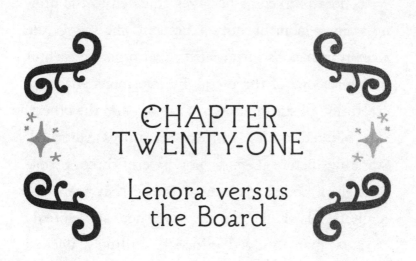

CHAPTER TWENTY-ONE

Lenora versus the Board

Lenora paused, looking up at the screaming Not-Director. Then another voice screamed over his: "Daddy!" And suddenly Ada flew into view, clinging to her father and sobbing.

At the sight of Ada, Lenora raced up the ladder herself, emerging into a large, round room lit dimly by thousands of candles. There were no windows anywhere to let in sunlight. The room was circled by a dozen or so pillared balconies stacked one on top of another, going all around except for three huge alcoves embedded in a semicircle in the wall.

Lenora blinked as her eyes adjusted to the dimness. For a moment, only a moment, she saw in the alcoves enormous thrones fifty feet high, on each of which sat one of three equally enormous shadowy creatures, all staring down at Lenora and the others. She blinked again, and the creatures vanished. Standing before Lenora now were three people (though of course, as Lenora knew, they were not really people at all). She had seen them all before:

A woman in a red raincoat, smiling a wicked smile.

A man in a green raincoat, grinning an evil grin.

A young girl in a long purple raincoat, baring hideous, sharp teeth.

Lenora shuddered. The Board had been right in front of her all along.

Lenora had only moments to take this all in before she was struck from the side. The projectile was Ada, who had hurled herself at Lenora, throwing her arms around her and screaming, "Lenora!" straight into her ear.

"Yes, yes, I'm here," said Lenora, struggling to

escape while her head swirled with no ideas at all on how to deal with these three creatures.

For his part, the Not-Director was somehow, again, recovering himself. He had stifled his screams and was patting down his hair and suit and struggling to change the expression on his face from fright to confidence. He jutted his chin out, frowned, and stabbed a finger at each member of the Board, one after the other.

"Now you listen to me," he said with command. "The only one who does any firing around here is me. I'm the smartest and make the best decisions. I'm the one in charge!"

The girl in the purple raincoat laughed sharply, a noise so piercing that Lenora almost clapped her hands over her ears. The girl ignored the Not-Director and addressed Lenora. "Yes," she said, her pointed red tongue flicking over those sharp teeth. "He's the one in charge, isn't he?"

"No," said Lenora with as much firmness as she could muster. "Not anymore."

"I am so!" cried the Not-Director. But there was uncertainty in his voice.

"His lies," said the girl, again to Lenora, "have lost their power. He is beginning to realize that, very slowly of course."

"Now just one minute—" started the Not-Director, but he was interrupted by the man in the green raincoat, who spoke only to Lenora.

"Do you not hate him?" said the man in a voice full of slime. "He destroyed your precious Library, after all."

"Well, I don't think, I, you know," the Not-Director sputtered. "That's not—"

"No," said Lenora to the man. "I don't hate him. He was only ever your tool."

"What a shame," sighed the man. "A girl such as you would have made a valuable ally."

"I'm not a tool!" yelled the Not-Director. But no one was listening. Even Ada had taken her place beside Lenora now, her hands curled into trembling fists.

"You get out of here!" Ada cried. "Leave us alone, or I'll—"

The woman in the red raincoat laughed. "You'll what? I can see the fear in all three of you. You know you cannot stand against us. We're going to devour all of you." Her nose wrinkled. "Well, maybe not *him*. He doesn't look very tasty. We'll just hurl him into a void outside of time and let him float there forever."

"No," whispered the Not-Director. "Please . . . not Prin—I mean, Ada . . . not my daughter . . . I'm—"

"No," shouted Ada, leaping in front of her father, tears streaming down her cheeks. "Please! Not my daddy. He can't hurt you!"

"No," said the woman. "He cannot." She gestured, and Ada was flung several feet through the air, hitting the floor with a hard thud.

"Ada!" Lenora ran to her, kneeling to place herself between Ada and the Board.

"Daddy," whispered Ada weakly. Both girls looked toward her father.

All three Board members had clenched their hands into fists, pointed straight at the Not-Director. Beneath his suit, things began slithering, things that he struck out at desperately, landing blows all over his body. His face turned red, then purple, and though his mouth was open wide, he made no sound.

A dark portal appeared, and with a thrust of the Board's fists, the Not-Director stumbled into it and vanished.

The portal started to close.

And too late, Lenora realized that Ada had gotten to her feet and was stumbling toward the shrinking portal, saying, "Daddy . . . Daddy . . . no . . ."

Lenora leapt to her feet and ran, reaching for Ada, pulling her back from the portal just before it vanished with a pop.

The Board began laughing, hideously and hysterically.

Lenora spun to face them. "Don't you dare hurt him!" she shouted.

"Oh, don't worry about him, little one," said the girl in purple.

"Yes," said the man in green, "we don't care about him. You are the one who ruined all our careful planning, all our decades of work."

"We have a special punishment for *you*," spat the woman in red.

The girl in purple grinned her sharp grin and held out her hands. The others took them.

Lenora took several steps back, as she had seen something like this once before. The Board members were melting into one another like candles, growing larger and larger. Soon they were one hideous person, six times the height of Malachi.

The monster grinned down at Lenora with a mouth full of razor-sharp teeth. Lenora looked everywhere for a weapon, but there was none to be found. When she turned back to the creature, it had changed.

It was a grotesque thing, composed of pure darkness, black eyes glittering. Shreds of its raincoats flapped in tatters on each side, and within the tatters, within the darkness, Lenora could see images rushing past like broken bits of a movie—the entire Library in ruins, ceilings caved in, walls fallen over, weeds winding through the rubble. Here and there she could see fires, hideous blazes with a horrid scent that stung Lenora's nose, and the Forces of Darkness rushing forward with books in their arms, hurling them into the blaze.

And all three members of the Board towered sixty feet over Lenora and Ada, standing all alone.

CHAPTER TWENTY-TWO
Lenora, Fear, and Lies

The monstrous creature towered over Lenora and Ada.

And towered. And towered. After a few moments of this, Lenora realized the monster had stopped moving. The flames in the images of burning books were no longer flickering. And beside her, Ada was frozen in place, her mouth opened to scream and her arms raised halfway over her head.

Everything had stopped. Everything except Lenora. She looked at her hands and flexed her fingers, then looked back up at the Board, wondering how this had happened and what she should do. And then she felt a presence behind her and turned.

"Malachi!" she cried.

For there stood the ~~Chief~~ Assistant Answerer.

The giant woman bent to one knee and reached down to take Lenora by the shoulder. And, for the first time Lenora had ever seen, she smiled.

"Yes, Lenora," said Malachi. "Now listen, for we have very little time. The Library is in full revolt. But here and now, the Forces of Darkness are many, and we are very few. I am needed elsewhere. It is up to you to defeat the Board."

"Defeat them how?" said Lenora with despair, for she had been sure that Malachi was here to accomplish that very thing. "I'm not powerful like you!"

"Really," said Malachi. "Was it I who found a place of safety for librarians to gather their strength? Was it I who saved Zenodotus from the depths of his sorrow, and exposed the Director, and created a rebel army that waited only for your command to strike? You are more powerful than you know, Lenora. And remember, as always—your friends are all around you. I asked one of them to lend you this, in fact." And into Lenora's hand she placed an object.

Lenora recognized it immediately. Rosa's device, the one they'd used to find the koala, and Zenodotus. But whatever would she do with this?

There was no time to ask. There was a blinding flash of light, so bright that Lenora closed her eyes. And when she opened them, Malachi was gone, and it appeared that she'd taken Ada with her, for Lenora was all alone. Except for the Board, who had returned to their human forms and were looking around frantically.

"What happened?" shouted the woman in the red raincoat.

The man in the green raincoat focused his gaze as though looking at something far away. "Librarians," he said, shocked. "Everywhere, all over the Library."

"That's impossible," spat the young girl in the long purple raincoat. Her tongue flicked out between her sharp teeth. "Where have they come from?"

"We must stop them—now!" cried the woman, and with three popping sounds, the Board vanished.

I have to follow them! thought Lenora. She gripped Rosa's location device and pictured the woman in the red raincoat.

Nothing happened.

She thought furiously. What had Rosa said? *I can locate anyone once I have their image.* But the image in Lenora's mind, of a woman in red, was of course not her true image. The woman had appeared as a huge, shadowy creature, too, and then again as a colossal dark nothingness. Lenora had no idea what her, or rather its, true form was.

If it even had one . . .

Lenora snapped her fingers.

The creature did have a true form. And it had been revealed when Lenora first met it. In fact, she had encountered this creature a number of times in her life, long before she had ever become a librarian.

And when Lenora had stood bolted to the floor, terrified, her words coming out in a squeak, she had remembered what Malachi taught her, and the creature had hissed and flinched, giving Lenora time to escape.

She gripped Rosa's device. She closed her eyes and remembered all the times in her life when she had been afraid, alone in the dark when she was very young, on her first day at a new school when she knew no one, and that terrible day when her parents told her that her grandmother had . . .

Wind nearly knocked her from her feet.

Lenora opened her eyes. She was no longer in the Board's chamber, but standing atop some domed structure high up in the sky, with wind gusting so terribly she had to drop to her hands and knees immediately to keep it from hurling her right off the edge. Terror surged through her as she thought, *I'm going to fall,* and imagined the horrible plunge awaiting her, even as she looked up and saw the woman in the red raincoat standing in the center of the dome, her arms raised, laughing. Lenora struggled to support herself on her trembling limbs, knowing she oughtn't be afraid. But the wind was still forcing her ever closer to the edge, scraping the skin off her hands and knees.

And she would fall. She was sure of it. She'd fall, and with that the Forces would take over the Library forever. She had failed. She tried to summon the strength to crawl forward, but could not. She felt one of her knees go off the edge into open air, and then—

"Lenora!"

Haruto shot past her. The boy was standing on some kind of disc that hovered in the air and seemed to be powered by something in his backpack, but Lenora didn't have time to think about that, for he was heading right for the woman in red, who shrieked and dodged, and for an instant her spell was broken and Lenora clawed her way back from the edge.

The woman recovered quickly and raced toward Lenora as Haruto flew in a circle around the dome. Lenora felt terror crash down over her once more. A moment later, the woman had Lenora by the arms, laughing, shoving her back toward the edge.

But this time, she thought, *I will not fall. Haruto will catch me.*

The woman's eyes flashed red in fury.

"I am not afraid!" shouted Lenora. "This is my Library, and my friends will always be here for me." And now she began to push, hard as she could, and this time it was the woman who took a step back.

With a final shriek, the woman transformed once more, briefly, into a creature of pure nothingness— and then, as though she were sucked away through a straw, she vanished.

There was no time to celebrate. Lenora waved to Haruto, cried, "Thank you!" over the roar of his hover board, and gripped Rosa's device. She remembered the lies the girl in the purple raincoat had told her. That Lenora had been fired, and Malachi had been devoured.

The windswept dome vanished.

Lenora found herself in a long, columned hallway, surrounded by a whirlwind of action. Everywhere, librarians were running up and down, some of them pushing empty bookshelves back into place along the walls or adding books to the shelves. Strangely, the walls were also covered with hundreds of signs that said things like:

WAR IS PEACE

FREEDOM IS SLAVERY

IGNORANCE IS STRENGTH

The phrases sounded like famous lines from a book whose title Lenora couldn't recall. But there was, again, no time to figure this out, for these were lies and Lenora knew the girl in purple must be responsible. She ripped some of the signs from one part of the wall, then another, but when she turned back, more signs had appeared.

Lenora caught a passing librarian by the arm. "What's going on?" she asked, gesturing at the signs.

"I don't know," said the harried librarian, who was lugging a box of books and looked quite weary. "We've tried tearing them down, but it's no good. Please, Lenora, do something!" She hurried away with her box. Lenora watched her go, allowing herself one moment of pride at how hard her fellow librarians were fighting. Then she turned her attention back to the matter at hand.

She looked everywhere, but she couldn't see the girl in purple. Patrons were gathering around the signs now, and some of them were beginning to nod. Lenora even saw a small boy writing in a notebook as he studied the signs.

How can they believe these lies? she thought. Then she noticed something happening to her, too. A tiny drumbeat in her head, repeating over and over, louder and louder: Ignorance is strength. IGNORANCE IS STRENGTH. IGNORANCE! IS! STRENGTH!

The lie began to make a certain sort of sense to Lenora. When repeated over and over like that, it seemed to become not a lie, but truth. She took out her notebook. And then—

"Lenora!"

Rosa came sailing toward her through the crowd.

"Rosa!" cried Lenora. Her wise and knowledge-able friend's appearance caused the awful drumbeat to cease immediately. "Thank goodness you've come."

"Malachi told all of your friends you would need us. What can I do?"

Lenora gestured to the signs again. "Someone is putting these up everywhere. They are having a very strange effect on patrons, and me! We need to remove them all and find her. I bet you've got an idea."

Rosa's helmet glittered in a way that suggested twinkling eyes. Rosa waved one of its many devices, and a whirlwind sprang up that ripped all the signs from the walls and gathered them into a spinning tornado of lies.

And in the middle of them stood a girl in purple, shock on her face.

She recovered quickly. Looking straight at Lenora, she said through her sharp teeth, "You have lost forever. Give up."

But Lenora shook her head. "Your lies won't work on me anymore. I see you for what you are. And know this—I will fight untruths wherever I find them, for as long as I'm able. And there will be

others like me who fight your lies, always, wherever you appear." Lenora knew this was true.

With a hiss, the girl began to transform into a
dark nothingness. And then, as though she were
being sucked away through a straw, she vanished.

"One more to go," said Lenora to Rosa. "And
then I can give you back your device. But quickly—
why are you here? I thought you were meeting
your spaceship."

"My ship is stuck here for the time being,"
replied Rosa. "The koala stole one of its parts!"

"That darn koala," said Lenora. "We'll get him
someday! Goodbye for now."

She gripped the device tightly, and thought once
more of the hatred and rage she had felt toward the
man in the green raincoat, and how she'd wanted
to attack him . . .

The hallway vanished.

CHAPTER
TWENTY-THREE
Lenora Leaves

For a moment, Lenora couldn't figure out where she was. It was as though she were in the middle of a gigantic factory that contained one huge machine. Everywhere she looked, she saw conveyor belts, platforms with spinning rollers, and slides that led down to wheeled buckets. There were even little robots scattered around the floor. But none of it, whatever it was, was operating. The robots and conveyor belts weren't moving at all. Lenora suspected that it ought to be working, but had no idea what to do about it. She hurried along, searching for the thing she had come for—the man in green, who seemed, in some ways, to be the worst of all the members of the Board.

As she went, she noticed there were openings all along the walls through which the belts moved (or ought to be moving). Above many of these doors were signs that read FOLKLORE and ALGEBRA and COSMOLOGY and hundreds of other topics. These were all library categories. Lenora was beginning to think this massive machine was all for sorting books. And then she saw something odd. Above one of the doors was a sign that said, simply, LENORA, in bold black letters.

No time to wonder, for she heard sounds ahead of her, and she sped up into a run. Veering around a silent conveyor belt, she ground to a halt.

She had found the man in green.

He was standing in front of an enormous vat of books, at least twenty stories high. It looked like the books were supposed to feed out onto the conveyor belts, but a door through which they moved had been slammed shut. In its place the man in the green raincoat had pulled up a trolley full of many different books, which he was preparing to dump onto the belts.

Lenora saw some of the titles. We will not repeat them here, but will only write a very sad thing. Some books exist that are not meant to educate, or entertain, or illuminate. They are meant to spread fear, lies, and hatred, and when read by those who do not understand their true purpose, they can be deadly things indeed.

Lenora knew these books for what they were, and hate rose within her. She found herself again wanting to throw herself at the man. Her fists shook.

He was looking right at her, and smiling. "I've reprogrammed this machine, you know. Now these books will be spread throughout the Library, instead of being kept in a special section just for them."

Before Lenora could move, the man dumped the books onto a belt and hit a button on a nearby control panel.

The machine started. Books of hate began moving down the belts. And then—

"Lenora!"

Ada shot into view. She had given up her out-
landish outfit and platform shoes, and for some
reason had dressed up in the costume of an old-
fashioned explorer. She threw herself into Lenora's
arms. "Lenora, Malachi told all your friends—"

"I know," replied Lenora. "Now Ada, please listen. This machine is supposed to sort all books into
their correct sections, but it's been reprogrammed.
I don't know how to fix it. I need you to do it, and
fast. I have to deal with this man."

"What man?" Ada asked.

Lenora turned. The man was gone. Then, out
of the corner of her eye, she spied a flash of green.
The man was running down one of the belts, and
he was out of sight a moment later.

"Quickly," she said to Ada. "I've got to go after
him. And you've got to fix this machine before any
of those books go out."

"But I've never seen it before," cried Ada in
despair. "Please, Lenora, stay and help me!"

Lenora held Ada by her arms and looked into
her eyes. "Ada, I will do my best, but I will not

always be there to help you. Know that you are braver and smarter than you realize, and you will find you do not need me as much as you think. Now hurry. We're out of time."

Ada gulped, tears in her eyes. Then she nodded and ran to the control panel.

Lenora jumped onto the conveyor belt and chased after the final member of the Board. She found that by running on the belts that were moving in the direction she wanted to go, she could move at blinding speed, and soon she caught up with the man, who had his back against a wall.

He turned to her, grinning. "You can never defeat us, you know. We might be silenced for a while, but we will always come back. Eventually we will win."

Lenora felt her hate for him returning. But now she understood this thing for what it was, and knew that she must not become that same thing.

So though it was difficult, she said calmly instead, "I remember how I felt outside the Director's office, when you and I first met." Though she supposed she had met this creature before, in other forms. "I hated you. And it was one of the most awful feelings I've ever had. How terrible it must be for you to feel that same way all the time. I'm very sorry for you."

At these words, the man howled terribly, and just as he began to turn into a dark nothingness, he was sucked away to wherever the others had gone.

"Fixed it!" she heard Ada yell.

The belt Lenora was standing on reversed, and she stumbled and fell.

Lenora could see right away that not only had Ada fixed the sorting machine, but it was now operating three times faster than before and it would be dangerous to stand on it. She had just managed to push herself into a seated position when the belt whooshed her onto a small platform and some spinning wheels came up and rolled her right onto another belt. All around, books on this and other belts were getting the same treatment, being pushed from belt to belt and then through doors in the walls marked ECOLOGY and GENETICS and FUNGI and every other topic one could possibly think of.

Lenora's belt roared toward a door in a wall and she found herself speeding along through a glass tunnel, and below her she could see a vast, sunlit reading room completely lined with tall bookshelves all along the walls, every one of them filled with books, and there were smiling librarians hurrying about, directing patrons to this or that. She could see all their faces, and on them she saw not one bit of fear or hatred, and she knew that every one of those patrons was being directed to books filled with truth, and warmth rushed through her as she realized: *We won*.

A moment later, Lenora shot through the end of the glass tunnel and onto another platform, only this time the platform began to rise through the air, and as she passed a window she could see onto the roof of a nearby building, across which ran a koala with a glittering object clutched in one paw as Rosa flew in pursuit.

Lenora couldn't see what happened next, for the platform continued upward. She passed another window, and now she was looking into another room, where she spotted Malachi giving some solemn instruction to Ada in her explorer's clothes, and the girl nodding gravely before stepping into a portal just like the one her father had vanished through.

That view disappeared as the platform continued upward. At last it stopped, and two robotic arms came out from the wall and turned Lenora gently so she was facing the opposite direction, and then more rollers sent her onto a new belt, and soon she was headed right for the door above which was written in bold black letters: LENORA.

And then she was tumbling down a steep slide, head over heels, until she fell through a small square portal that instantly slid shut behind her. It slid shut so perfectly that where there had once been a door, you could not now tell there had been anything but a wall. She looked about and saw that she had been sorted back to exactly where a Lenora should be—behind the information desk of a wonderful library with lovely, large windows through which sunlight poured eagerly in, and beautiful cedar beams that stretched up to the high ceiling. She had just gotten to her feet and dusted herself off when she heard a woman's sharp voice from around the corner:

"I tell you, that girl has been gone for ten minutes now! We're leaving!"

And a boy's voice replied:

"Please, just a little longer!"

Lenora raced around the corner toward the boy who was waiting for an answer about the world's largest number, and soon she would tell him all about Milton Sirotta and TREE(3) and Graham's number, and that even bigger numbers might be found by someone armed with the light of knowledge, and after that he would stagger with a smile from the library under the weight of a stack of math books Lenora had chosen for him, and as she watched him go she would smile happily, too, for on her chest over her heart was a new badge, a badge with words that were simple but summed up everything:

And she knew, she knew . . .

SHE
WOULD
ALWAYS
BE
BACK!

ACKNOWLEDGMENTS

Rebel in the Library of Ever may never have become known to the world had Paige Wheeler and her team of daredevils at Creative Media Agency not rappelled into the cavern where the manuscript had been hidden and brought it forth into the light. They smuggled it to John Morgan at Imprint, whose editorial wisdom shaped it into the book you are holding today. Matt Rockefeller knocked everyone out with his visionary cover, giving us a portrait of Lenora for which Zeno will be forever grateful. Erin Stein's editorial insights were also invaluable. Morgan Rath, Dawn Ryan, Regina Castillo, Jie Yang, and Carolyn Bull performed heroic work as well. And Zeno would have no books at all without his first reader, Miriam Angress, now and forever. The assistance of the brilliant authors of Adverb Fight Club (John Claude Bemis, Jennifer Harrod, and JJ Johnson) is grand without measure. And of course, the utmost gratitude to Lenora, who allowed Zeno to tell her story.

ACKNOWLEDGMENTS

Zeno may be reached via electronic post
at zenoalexander@pm.me, or on Twitter @
ZAlexanderBooks.

ABOUT THE AUTHOR

After emerging from the shadows of the past, his history yet to be fully explained, **Zeno Alexander** spent years exploring the world's libraries before settling down in his lavish underground bunker, where he regularly hosts exquisite dinner parties and tends to his collection of extinct plants. His friendship with the famous librarian Lenora has turned into a series of biographical works devoted to chronicling her adventures.